NANCY DREW® 167

MYSTERY BY MOONLIGHT

CAROLYN KEENE

D1023562

Aladdin Paperbacks
New York   London   Toronto   Sydney   Singapore

If you purchased this book without a cover, you should be aware that this book is stolen property. It was reported as "unsold and destroyed" to the publisher and neither the author nor the publisher has received any payment for this "stripped book."

This book is a work of fiction. Any references to historical events, real people, or real locales are used fictitiously. Other names, characters, places, and incidents are the product of the author's imagination, and any resemblance to actual events or locales or persons, living or dead, is entirely coincidental.

First Aladdin Paperbacks edition July 2002

Copyright © 2002 by Simon & Schuster, Inc.

ALADDIN PAPERBACKS
An imprint of Simon & Schuster
Children's Publishing Division
1230 Avenue of the Americas
New York, NY 10020

All rights reserved, including the right of
reproduction in whole or in part in any form.

Manufactured in the United States of America

10 9 8 7

NANCY DREW and NANCY DREW MYSTERY STORIES are registered trademarks of Simon & Schuster, Inc.

Library of Congress Control Number: 2001097942

ISBN-13: 978-0-7434-3762-2
ISBN-10: 0-7434-3762-4

Contents

1	A Cry in the Night	1
2	Too Many Neighbors	7
3	Dangerous Curve	18
4	Burgled	33
5	The Uninvited Guest	46
6	A Killer Storm	57
7	A Secret Revealed	65
8	Blinded by the Light	72
9	What Lies Above	81
10	The Best Laid Plans	91
11	A Familiar Prowler	104
12	Shadows in the Moonlight	111
13	Drowning in Moonlight	122
14	A Ghostly Fleet	130
15	The Past Revealed	139

1

A Cry in the Night

Late one August night, Nancy Drew drove along a twisting dirt road with the top of her Mustang convertible down, and a smile on her face. Stars glittered above her head. The forest alongside the road was fragrant after an earlier shower. The breeze was warm, and Nancy felt comfortable without a sweater over her strappy blue tank top.

Nancy and her boyfriend, Ned Nickerson, had been traveling since dawn, sharing the long drive from River Heights to the Pocono Mountains of eastern Pennsylvania. But even though it was past midnight, Nancy was wide-awake and eager to catch her first glimpse of Moonlight Lake, where her friends George Fayne and Bess Marvin were house-sitting for George's cousin Jason and his wife, Jennifer.

1

Nancy glanced across the front seat at Ned. He was studying a sheet of paper by the narrow beam of Nancy's penlight.

"What's our next landmark?" she asked.

"Says, 'A stack of three white mailboxes on the left. Hard to find!'" Ned grinned at Nancy. "As if anything since we turned off the interstate has been *easy* to find."

Nancy laughed, then spotted the mailboxes in the car's headlights. The mailboxes were covered with some sort of vines. As Nancy slowed down and turned onto the narrow gravel drive, she said, "I hope all that green stuff isn't poison ivy!"

"Whoever has this mail route probably hopes so too," Ned said with a laugh.

Nancy concentrated on the road. The driveway was in bad shape, and overshadowed by thick hemlock trees. After the first ten feet or so, it pitched steeply downhill, then it suddenly opened out, branching off in three different directions.

"It's the middle driveway," Ned instructed as Nancy slowed down. A larger drive cut off to the right, while another small dirt road, barely wider than a footpath, led to the left into the heart of the hemlock forest. But just ahead at the bottom of the hill, the trees thinned out, and Nancy caught her first glimpse of Moonlight Lake.

Nancy braked to a stop and let the car idle as she

2

drank in the view. The setting was romantic, even more beautiful than George had made it sound last week when she invited Ned and Nancy to spend time at the cottage. A light breeze lifted Nancy's thick reddish-blond hair off her shoulders. Her blue eyes sparkled with delight. What a perfect place for the last fling of what had been a really great summer!

"Did you order up the nearly-full moon for the occasion, Nan?" Ned teased. Nancy released the brake and slowly continued down the drive toward a small two-storied stone cottage perched on the edge of the lake. The porch lights were on. Music and the smell of brownies baking wafted out the screen door.

Before Nancy could answer Ned's question, a figure burst from the door and jogged up to the car, flashlight in hand.

"Nancy!" Bess's familiar voice called as Nancy was pulling into the driveway next to an old station wagon. "Am I ever glad to see you!" she declared.

"That's good, since we plan to spend the week here," Ned joked as he climbed out of the car and stretched his arms over his head.

Nancy put up the top of the car and popped the trunk before getting out. She and Bess hugged, then Nancy held her friend at arm's length. Although Bess's smile was wide, her blue eyes looked worried.

"Is something wrong?" Nancy asked.

"I'm not sure," Bess said. "But things are getting

definitely weird around here lately."

"What's going on?" Nancy prodded, arching her eyebrows. "George didn't mention anything when we spoke on the phone last night."

Bess gave an exasperated sigh. "Oh, you know George. Sometimes she is so levelheaded, it's disgusting." Nancy smiled. George and Bess were first cousins and devoted friends, but in everything from looks to interests, they might as well have been born on different planets.

Nancy listened patiently as Bess continued. "I'm positive George has heard the same noises I have almost every night. There's a ghost, Nancy—a real ghost that's haunting this place. Until today I thought it was the ghost of someone murdered on this very spot!" Bess jerked her head toward the cottage. She lowered her voice to a whisper. "But now I'm sure it's the restless spirit of a child left behind and drowned when the valley was flooded back in the twenties to form the lake!"

"I don't like the sound of this," Ned said with mock seriousness. "We came for a vacation, and already you have Nancy on the case, tracking down some drowned ghost."

"Well it's true! I know—"

"Because it's in the paper," George finished for Bess as she approached the car. She aimed her flashlight at the small pile of luggage Ned had already extracted from the trunk. "Hi Nan, Ned. Great to see you. You'll be happy to know you're just in time for brownies."

"And ghost stories around the campfire! What more could a guy want!" Ned joked.

"Laugh all you want, but it's true," Bess insisted. "George read the same story I did, but she just doesn't believe it."

"I think it's just a feature story to lure tourists to the area," George maintained.

Nancy stifled a smile. Bess was serious, and Nancy didn't want to hurt her feelings. "What did the paper say?" Nancy asked.

George answered for Bess. "Oh, there was an article commemorating the anniversary of the hydroelectric project that created this lake back in the Prohibition era. The article had quotes from locals who swear that the spirits of former area residents still frequent the lakeshore houses."

"Power of suggestion," Ned said, shouldering two duffle bags and starting toward the back porch. "All old houses have noises."

"Not like these!" Bess declared with a vigorous shake of her head.

"What kind of noises?" Nancy asked, looking at George.

"Weird ones," George readily admitted.

"Screams," Bess added. "And that creaking at

5

night in the ceiling. . . ." Bess shuddered.

"Mice in the attic," Ned said firmly. "Just mice."

"Except there *is* no attic!" George pointed out. "And Bess is right about one thing—the noises are seriously freaky. Still, there has to be some rational explanation for them."

"In your dreams, maybe," Bess scoffed. But her next words were cut off by a woman's scream. It was high and piercing and made Nancy's skin crawl.

"What was *that*?" Nancy gasped.

"The ghost—it's the ghost!" Bess cried in a panic. "And it's coming this way!" she shrieked.

There was a sound of something crashing through the forest. Nancy turned. Whatever had screamed was plunging toward them. Suddenly a huge, dark shape broke through the underbrush and into the yard.

"It's no ghost!" Nancy gasped at the sight of the large, furry creature coming toward her. "It's a—"

Nancy never got to finish her sentence. The huge creature threw itself against her, pinning her to the ground.

"It's a bear!" Bess wailed, making a beeline for the porch.

6

2

Too Many Neighbors

A scream rose to Nancy's lips, but her cry was smothered by the huge beast.

"A bear! A bear!" she heard Bess scream.

This thing is not heavy enough to be a bear! Nancy thought as she struggled to squirm out from under the wriggling mass of fur. She pushed with all her might, and her hand gripped its fuzzy pelt. Then her fingers closed on something else. It was smooth and cool and studded with some kind of metal balls. It felt like a . . . a *collar*! Nancy grasped it, and suddenly a big wet tongue began licking her face. She managed to roll out from beneath the creature.

"It's a dog!" George gasped, helping Ned pull the huge dog off Nancy.

Nancy scrambled to her feet and began to laugh.

"Stop it, you silly dog!" she commanded as Ned dragged the dog away. The dog wagged its tail and turned its affections toward Ned, jumping up and planting its massive paws on his shoulders. With great enthusiasm, it began to lick Ned's neck.

Laughing, Ned tried to push the dog down while Nancy rubbed her hip where she had fallen. "Are you okay?" he asked.

"I'll survive," Nancy said. She could see in the light spilling from the porch that the dog was some sort of mixed breed—part Newfoundland, part . . . something very furry. Its coat was black and studded with burrs and all sorts of leaf litter. "Just scraped my elbow when Bigfoot here tackled me!"

"Down, boy, down!" Ned ordered, letting go of the dog's collar. The dog obeyed, sitting erect at Ned's feet. He looked up expectantly at Ned, his fluffy tail thumping the ground. Ned looked surprised. "It's sure not a stray—someone's trained it."

"Not well enough," George grumbled, helping Nancy dust off her jeans.

"You're sure it's just a dog? Like, not part wolf or something?" Bess called from the safety of the porch. She sounded skeptical.

"Definitely a dog," Nancy said, grabbing some paper towels from the trunk of her car and wiping her face. "Definitely big. Definitely affectionate." She turned toward George. "Where did it come

8

from?" she asked. "Do you know its name?"

George shook her head. "I've never seen this guy before," she said, crouching down and patting the dog. Nancy dropped down next to her and began gently removing the burrs from its fur.

"So, we don't know whose dog it is," Nancy stated.

"Or who screamed!" Bess pointed out, cautiously approaching the dog and reaching out her hand to let him sniff her fingers.

The dog nuzzled Bess's hand. Suddenly, it lifted its head and stared intently into the woods. A second later it jumped to its feet and started barking furiously. Just as it prepared to bolt into the trees, Ned snared the dog by the collar. "Hold it!" Ned shouted as he spotted a woman coming out of the brush.

She strode toward them, the beam of her flashlight bobbing against the scruffy grass. She was tall and gangly, and Nancy was surprised to see her dressed in a long-sleeved camouflage shirt and camouflage trousers. Weird outfit for this time of night, she thought.

"Is this your dog?" the woman asked Nancy in a strong British accent. She looked furious.

Before Nancy could reply, a man broke through the brush, carrying a battery-operated lantern. He was only slightly taller than the woman, and wiry with a beaklike nose and a thin face. Like the woman, he was dressed all in camouflage.

9

"This is the last straw!" the man fumed. "You'd better keep this dog leashed, or I'm calling the police. Enough is enough!"

Nancy frowned and exchanged a quick glance with George. George looked as annoyed and perplexed as Nancy felt. "I'm sorry about the dog, Caspar, but I haven't a clue where he's from," George told the man sharply. She introduced the middle-aged couple to Nancy and Ned. "This is Millicent and Caspar Lawrence-Jones. They're our neighbors on the next lakefront property." Turning back to the couple, George said, "These are my friends Nancy Drew and Ned Nickerson. They're here for the week."

Millicent gave Nancy an exasperated look. "Great. More kids, more partying—and loud goings-on. Glad to meet you."

"We didn't come to throw loud parties!" Nancy said in her defense.

"So if this isn't *your* dog," Caspar Lawrence-Jones said to George, "whose is it?"

George shrugged. "Beats me. I've never seen him before."

Nancy crouched down and tickled the dog's ears as she looked to see if there was anything written on his collar.

Just then the sound of an approaching motorcycle made everyone turn. The dog let out a happy yip, then bounded down the side of the driveway toward the approaching headlight. "Hey, Tiny, watch out!" a gruff voice called. A moment later the owner of the voice came into view.

He was a stocky man who seemed too big for his motorcycle. He was wearing flip-flops, baggy shorts, and a black T-shirt emblazoned with a Camp Moonlight logo. The word "Chief" was inscribed on his baseball cap, and a tattoo of a crescent moon peeked out from under the short sleeve of his shirt.

"Tiny, how'd you ever get loose?" The man stopped the bike, and the dog leaped all over him. "Down, now. Behave yourself."

Tiny instantly sat down and looked adoringly at his master's face.

"Is this *your* dog?" Caspar asked angrily.

"Yeah. What of it?" the man shot back.

"What of it?" Bess repeated incredulously. She marched right up to the man and said, "He practically killed my friend Nancy, here."

"It wasn't as bad as that!" Nancy interjected quickly. She wasn't sure she liked the looks of this guy on the motorcycle, and she didn't want to pick a fight with him.

"It was more than bad for us!" Millicent fumed. "That dog ruined a whole night's work."

Nancy looked at George. "Work?" she mouthed.

George arched her eyebrows and nodded as

11

Caspar went on. "More like two weeks work. We've been trying to get some footage of a gray owl attacking its prey. Just when the owl spotted the bait, your dumb mutt homed in on the bait and knocked down our setup."

"He's not dumb!" the man said defensively, revving his bike. "What was the bait? A rabbit? Dogs hunt rabbits around these parts, mister." He looked at his dog. "Come on, Tiny, we're heading home."

"You'd better keep him leashed," Caspar threatened.

"Or what?" the man countered, wheeling his motorcycle around. "Look, he got loose. It's no big deal. He wouldn't hurt a soul." With that, the man gunned his engine and tore back up the drive, Tiny running behind him.

"What a piece of work!" Caspar said, staring after the bike's rear bumper light as it receded up the steep driveway, around a curve, and out of sight.

Millicent blew out her breath in a huff. "He's a rude, inconsiderate person. I thought that since his campers left this weekend, things would quiet down. Between the dog and—" She glared at Ned and Nancy and cut herself off. "C'mon, Caspar, let's grab our equipment and head back to the house. We've got to rebuild our rig first thing in the morning." The couple stomped back through the brush toward the forest.

"Uh, good night," Ned called after them.

"Right!" Caspar said, not bothering to turn around.

A frown crossed Nancy's face, but a moment later she shrugged and smiled. "Charming neighbors!" she joked.

Bess rolled her eyes. "Those two have been real pills ever since we got here. When Jason and Jennifer asked us to house-sit, I think the Lawrence-Joneses decided to hate us because we're eighteen-year-olds."

"Which to them means loud, wild parties," George added.

"Which, needless to say," Bess pointed out sadly, "isn't the case." She grabbed one of Nancy's bags and headed across the grass toward the back porch. "You know, I could use a party," she added.

"And I think *they* deserve a particularly loud one!" Ned suggested with a wicked gleam in his eye.

"Can't," George said. "I promised Jen and Jason we'd keep a low profile. Not embarrass them or anything. Though I'm sorely tempted. Besides, the Lawrence-Joneses may act completely obnoxious, but they're pretty interesting people."

"If you call grubbing around in the dark and baiting owls with dead rabbits interesting. I call it *gross*!" Bess commented as they headed through the back door of the stone cottage, through a small mudroom, and into the kitchen. "But compared to that Steve Delmonico, they're downright friendly."

"Steve Delmonico—is that the guy with the dog?" Ned asked.

"Yeah, he owns the summer camp next to the large house to the right of this cottage. He's freaked out that Emily bought the land out from under him when he wanted to expand his camp," George told them.

"Who's Emily?" Nancy asked, following Bess into the house.

"She's pretty cool. You'll meet her tomorrow," Bess said. "She lives in the house across the lawn, full-time. This cottage used to be a guest house on a larger estate before the property was divided up. Emily just moved in at the beginning of the summer." She motioned around the Fayne family cottage. "This is, of course, the kitchen. The kitchen and the family room is all there is downstairs—except for the deck. All the bedrooms are on the second floor."

Nancy surveyed the kitchen. It was old-fashioned, with appliances that looked like they were from the fifties. "Hannah would feel right at home here," Nancy remarked, referring to the housekeeper who had lived with her and her father ever since Nancy's mother had died.

"Especially with the pantry! You'll have to check it out later. Jennifer's developed the same passion as Hannah for canning fruits and veggies during her vacations here," George told Nancy as she put four tall glasses on a tray. "I don't get it—I couldn't stay inside the house, sweating over a hot stove in the summer. Not when there's so much else to do outdoors."

"Jen's the homey type," Bess remarked.

A pitcher of iced tea was on the metal-topped table in the center of the room, and brownies cooled on a rack on top of the chipped white enamel stove. "This place is great," Nancy said, "and those brownies smell good!"

"Take some, and pour yourself some tea. You probably need to unwind after such a long drive," Bess said, putting the brownies on a plate.

"I'm past dead already," Ned said. "The minute my head hits the pillow, I'm going to be out like a light. And I want to get up early and check out the lake. But no way this guy's turning down one of your brownies, Bess."

"I'm still too revved up to sleep!" Nancy declared, looking around the kitchen. She spotted a tray propped against the wall by the sink. Grabbing it, she loaded it with the pitcher of tea, the glasses, napkins, and a plate of brownies. "Let's take this out to the deck—unless there are too many mosquitoes."

"Nope—Jason's first purchase for the cottage was one of those bug zappers!" George said, as Ned opened the screen door for Nancy.

"Which, vile as they are, at least repel bugs." Bess

wrinkled her nose and looked distastefully at the bug-repellent device. It cast an eerie purple light over one corner of the deck.

Nancy put the tray on a round picnic table. The four friends grabbed their drinks, brownies, and napkins and settled down in the wood chairs. For a moment they were silent.

"What we really need around here," Bess said, pouring herself more iced tea, "is some sort of ghost repellent!"

"Here we go again!" George groaned, propping her feet up against the deck's railing.

"Because you sleep like a log, you don't hear the noises that go on out here on the lake, in the woods, and in the walls of the house!" Bess reminded her.

"There was a scream before," Ned conceded. "I heard it—though I'm sure it wasn't a ghost. It was probably that Millicent woman freaked out by the dog—what was its name?"

"Tiny!" Bess, Nancy, and George all answered at once, dissolving into giggles.

"Seriously, Bess," Nancy said as the laughter died down, "it's possible that if those people do research at night, they might be making the noises you hear. . . ."

"In the house?" Bess scoffed.

"You could always ask them," Ned suggested.

"No way," George said. "They aren't very friendly,

in case you hadn't noticed. The less we have to do with them, the better."

Nancy gazed out over the water, a smile playing across her lips. Leave it to Bess to get herself so worked up over ghosts. Suddenly out of the corner of her eye, she saw a movement. She turned and looked to her right. Puddles of light splashed the surface of the water, but closer to shore it was black as a shadow. Nancy leaned forward and shielded her eyes from the low light of the deck lanterns. As her vision adjusted to the dark, she was sure she saw a darker shadow slide through the dark waters near the shore.

"Nancy!" Bess cried, a note of fear in her voice. "What are you looking at?"

Nancy motioned for Bess to be quiet. "I'm not sure," Nancy whispered. "But I think someone or *something* is out there on the water!"

3

Dangerous Curve

"What kind of *something*?" Bess gasped.

Nancy shook her head and leaned farther over the railing. Ned, George, and Bess joined her.

"I don't see anything," Ned said.

Nancy frowned, still straining to distinguish between the shadows playing on the water near shore. "Me either, anymore. I'm sure something was in the water. It was long—like a boat, or a canoe, or maybe even some kind of big lake otter or beaver. Do you have them here?" She turned to face George, and a noise on the back porch made her jump.

"Someone's here!" Nancy cried, turning around quickly.

"Knock, knock," a light, pleasant female voice called

through the back screen door. "You guys all right?"

Bess sagged against George. "Oh, it's only Emily!" she said with obvious relief.

"We're out here on the deck," George called.

"Late night party?" the girl asked.

The back door squeaked open, and Nancy saw a young woman come into the kitchen and cross the family room.

Emily stood hesitantly on the other side of the deck's screen doors. Though she stifled a yawn as she walked up to Nancy, she looked perfectly wide-awake.

"I heard some sort of major ruckus going on over here and got worried. I thought maybe Steve's dog was hassling you guys—since hassling me doesn't seem to be working!" she said.

"That's not exactly what happened, but thanks for checking. Actually, we just thought we saw someone down on the lake," George told her.

"On the lake? At this hour?" Emily stepped onto the deck. "Unless Steve's got some new trick up his sleeve, I doubt it."

"Maybe it was just an animal . . . a beaver," Nancy suggested. "And by the way, I'm Nancy Drew, and this is my friend Ned Nickerson."

Emily put out her hand. "Emily Griffen, here. Bess and George mentioned you guys were coming for the week. That should set off the Lawrence-Joneses! They positively cringe at the sight of anyone under thirty!" She laughed, and two deep dimples appeared on her cheeks.

"So have you seen night animals on the lake?" Nancy asked.

Emily shrugged. "Actually, I'm not much of a night person myself. But there *are* beavers around here. I don't know if they swim around the lake at night. I was asleep when I heard the noise." She glanced around the deck, then out over the lake, then back across the yard toward the woods. "Everything seems quiet around here, so I'll head back. I was about ready to call the cops!"

"No need for that," Nancy assured her.

"Want to take a brownie with you?" Bess offered.

Emily shook her head. "Thanks, but I'm going back to bed. I'll take you up on your offer tomorrow, though, if there are any left."

Bess saw Emily out, and George brought the tray back into the kitchen, with Nancy and Ned close behind. "Your room is at the end of the hall, Ned. Nancy's is at the top of the stairs," George said. Ned started up the steps with the bags.

"That was sweet of Emily to head over here right away when she thought there was trouble," Bess said as she began putting the food away.

George looked up from the sink where she was

washing the glasses. "'Right away' isn't how I'd put it. It took her a while to get here."

"She was asleep," Nancy said absently. "Though that girl's beyond lucky. She sure doesn't wake up with bed-head!"

"You can say that again," Bess said with a sigh. Bess's hair was silky and straight and tended to look a major mess in the mornings.

"And did you see her shoes?" George laughed.

"Shoes and socks!" Nancy said.

"Of course *you'd* be the one to notice that," Bess teased. Nancy's keen eye seldom missed any details.

"It *is* sort of weird to be freaked out about noises over here, and then take the time to put on shoes and socks," George commented. "I'd race out barefoot— or, at the most, grab my flip-flops."

"To each his own," Nancy said with a yawn. "She seems like a nice neighbor."

"I like her. She apparently freelances as a TV journalist making documentaries, so she's usually buried in work. But maybe now that you guys are around, we can convince her to hang out with us more," Bess said. "We're going to town tomorrow; I'll ask her to come along."

After a leisurely late breakfast on the deck, the four friends piled into Nancy's Mustang and headed back toward Lost Valley, the small town that serviced

21

the lakeside community. Despite Bess's invite, Emily didn't join them.

It was the last week in August, just before Labor Day, and the village was busy. Nancy cruised Main Street twice, finally settling for a parking space at a meter in front of the town square. As she tucked her keys in the pocket of her shorts, she remarked, "Weird. This place didn't always have a lake, but those big houses on the hill are pure Victorian." She turned to George. "Did the village ever have another name?"

"Yeah," George replied, pointing to a bronze historic marker planted in the grass a few feet away. "The whole story's here. The town used to be called Lenape. The stream that was dammed up to flood the valley was Lenape Creek. About five years after the power company created the new lake, people voted to rename the town, since Lenape Creek didn't exist anymore."

"Weren't the Lenape an Indian tribe?" Nancy asked.

Bess nodded. "They still are. There's a small reservation just to the north of town. Apparently, the tribal activists want to go back to the old name of the town. Originally the tribe was so angered by the creation of the dam, they didn't want their name associated with the town."

"Meanwhile, they're also in court trying to reclaim

some of the sacred burial grounds around the lake," George added.

"The marker says the valley was a sparsely populated farm community," Ned pointed out, shaking his head. "But I bet the people whose pioneer forefathers settled the area found it hard to lose their land."

Nancy looked thoughtful. "It must have been difficult for all the residents of the valley to lose their homes."

"But that was a long time ago!" George reminded them, stopping to shake a pebble out of her sandal. "And Lost Valley has become a pretty successful tourist town. From what I've seen in the paper, no one, except for the hardcore Lenape activists, wants to see the lake drained and the valley restored, even if it were possible. This place is the biggest tourist and vacation attraction this end of the Poconos."

As they started toward the center of town, Nancy could see George's point. The stores lining Main Street looked prosperous, busy, and inviting.

Bess managed to move past most of the shops. "We can come back and explore all these places another day, if you guys want," Bess told them as she approached a large corner store. Outside were benches, big brown wooden pickle barrels, and a sign announcing that their iced tea was fresh-brewed and very cold. "This is the General Store. We've been shopping here instead of out at the big super-market in the mall, even though it costs a little more. It's way more fun!"

With that, she opened the double screen door and marched in. Nancy and the others followed. Even after she pocketed her sunglasses, it took a moment for Nancy to adjust to the interior light. The store's wood paneling gleamed. Shelves lining the wall were crammed with everything from jeans, work-clothes, and work boots, to toys and hardware. One area held a wide selection of canned and packaged grocery items. As Nancy's eyes adjusted, she saw there was a butcher counter at the back of the store, and another large area devoted to hunting and fishing supplies and other sports gear. An oval counter in the center of the room was lined with jars of candy and novelties, and the aroma of fresh-brewed coffee filled the air.

"Cool," Ned commented, heading straight for the hardware department. George started in the same general direction, making a beeline for the sporting gear, but Bess suddenly gripped her arm.

"Look," she gasped. Both George and Nancy turned in the direction of Bess's gaze. Bess was pointing at a lean dark-haired guy who stood against the counter, talking to the cashier. The man had high cheekbones, and was very good-looking.

Here goes Bess! Nancy thought, and smiled to herself.

"Isn't he the Lenape Native American rights activist whose picture was in the paper the other day? No way are there *two* of anyone that cute around!" Bess said, her eyes sparkling.

George took a couple of steps in the direction of the counter, studied the guy for a minute, then turned to Bess. "You're right," she said. "He's the one who works at the Native American museum on the other side of the town square. What was his name?"

"Jim something!" Bess remembered. "I'm going to scope him out." With that, Bess smoothed her hair, stopped to check her reflection in a mirror beside a display of baseball caps, then walked nonchalantly toward the counter.

Nancy and George exchanged a knowing glance. "While she's appreciating the local scenery, I'm going to see what's new in swimming gear," George said.

"Go ahead. I'll keep an eye on Bess," Nancy promised, casually making her way toward the counter. She didn't want to cramp her friend's style, but she too found something compelling about the guy. He had a focused, intense air about him. She wondered what he did at that museum.

She moved close enough to overhear Bess's conversation, but pretended to rifle through a rack of marked-down western-style cowboy shirts.

Nancy could see the guy was definitely flirting back at Bess. He had straightened up at her approach and was fingering the strand of small beads that he wore around his neck. He looked interested in whatever Bess was saying. Nancy strained to get the gist of their conversation.

"Wow, so you're an assistant curator at the museum?" Bess said, her blue eyes wide with admiration.

The guy smiled shyly. "Yeah. I got the job last January right after graduation from Penn State."

Nancy could practically hear the wheels inside Bess's head turning, figuring out exactly how old this Jim person was. Probably twenty-one or twenty-two—which was fine with Bess, who often dated guys as old as twenty-five.

"So, you like it around here?" Bess asked, tossing her hair back from her face.

The guy shrugged. "What's not to like? I've lived here forever. My whole family has lived up on the res. I don't live there myself these days. I've got my own place just outside of town. Where are you from?"

"The Midwest," Bess told him. "River Heights, to be exact. My cousin and I are house-sitting a cottage for the month over on Moonlight Lake. Maybe you know the place. It's on the north shore, and it used to be the guest cottage for the old Malone house."

"Yeah, I know the Malone house." The guy's expression darkened. "Right—I might have expected as much. Enjoy the cottage if you can." He made it sound like a challenge. With that he tossed some coins on the counter, grabbed a donut off a tray on the counter, and stalked past Nancy toward the front door. As he passed Nancy she saw that he wore an intricately beaded bracelet similar to the necklace and had a hunting knife in a leather case attached to his belt.

Nancy frowned as he slammed the screen door behind him. "What was that about?" she asked, walking up to Bess.

The color in Bess's cheeks had deepened from pink to an embarrassed red. "Beats me!" she said tightly. "Was he coming on to me or what? Then the next minute . . . it's like I have the plague."

"Maybe he has a grudge against the people who used to own the Malone house," Nancy suggested.

"Whatever!" Bess said with a proud toss of her head. She grabbed a handful of gummy candies, put them on the scale, and paid the proprietor a dollar. "Let's get out of here. I wanted to check out the junk store near here."

"I'm game," said Nancy, who loved rummaging in secondhand shops with Bess. "Though I think we might lose George and Ned."

"What's this about trying to lose us?" Ned said, walking up.

27

"We're not trying to lose you, but we're about to head to another store," Nancy explained as she and Bess turned to leave.

"Hey, I'm in." Ned shrugged. "I like this town. It's interesting. Find anything?" he asked as George came over.

"No, but the sales clerk told me to try the sports store at the other end of Main Street for the kind of goggles I want. He says they don't keep inventory up at this time of the summer, and there's been a run on the diving gear they do carry here. Meanwhile, I picked up some groceries for lunch and for tonight. Let me pay, then we'll head off." As George dug around in her purse, she asked as an afterthought, "So, was that him?"

"Yeah, and he's not much to brag about," Bess grumbled. Then she gave George a smile. "So it's a deal. We'll go to the junk shop first, and then the sports store."

"That's cool with me," George said. "I heard they do a lot of salvage around here. A junk shop might be just the place to see some really cool old farm implements from the nineteen-twenties before the valley was flooded. Besides, the goggles can wait. I shouldn't spend the money on them now, anyway."

George paid for the groceries, and a few minutes later the foursome was investigating Timothy's Trash and Treasures. The short gravel drive leading to the old barn was filled with items ranging from rusted metal bedsteads to delicate porcelain washbasins and wood-framed mirrors.

Inside, Nancy expected chaos. Instead, everything was in order. Books, magazines, and cases full of old maps were relegated to one area of the barn. Wooden crates full of housewares were stacked near the door. Glass cases displayed an enticing array of old jewelry, and garment racks bulged with retro clothes: sequined evening gowns from the Prohibition era hung next to scruffy furs.

The display of old maps caught Nancy's attention. While she was examining a framed Revolutionary War era chart, she overheard the owner talking with Bess.

"That there is a real nice example of a nineteen-twenties toaster."

Nancy peered over Bess's shoulder. Bess was holding a strange flat appliance that once was probably shiny metal but now was heavily rusted. It had a hinged flap that looked like a drop-down door on each side.

"That looks familiar," George said, joining them. "We have one of those back home in the attic. It's a toaster that belonged to my great-grandmother. Except ours still has the cord."

"Well, this thing's cord's been long gone. Someone

brought it in with a pile of other things that washed up from the lake."

"So, there really is salvage from the lake," Ned said.

"Not exactly salvage. Regular salvage operations are illegal at the moment, thanks to some court injunction in place until a suit between the landowners and the Lenape tribe is settled in court. But stuff that washes up on the shoreline"—the proprietor shrugged—"that's finders keepers. By the way, I'm Tim." He plunked himself down on a milk crate, seeming glad for the company. "There's been a lot of stuff this season. More than usual. Guess it had to do with a spell of stormy weather this past spring. A guy comes in from time to time with cartons of junk like this."

"Good for business," Ned remarked. "Though it's weird things are still washing up from last spring."

"I'm not complaining," Tim admitted. "Hey, the lake's got her moods, and now and then she gives up her secrets. Tourists jump at old junk supposedly dating back to before the creek was dammed up. Most of it's more recent than that—just usual garbage."

"Do you remember the valley before it was flooded?" Nancy asked.

"No, miss, that was before my time—I was born a couple of years after they created Moonlight Lake. But I have lived here my whole life."

"So I guess you've heard the ghost stories," Bess said.

Tim's eyes twinkled. "Guess I have. Some folks around here think they're just nonsense. Other folks swear they're the honest truth."

"And you?" Nancy asked.

Tim frowned. "Can't say for sure."

Ned chuckled. "Sounds like people keep the stories alive just to make Moonlight Lake more interesting."

"There *are no ghosts*!" George said firmly.

"Oh," Tim drawled, "I wouldn't be so sure of that. Once upon a time I thought it was all just a lot of bunk. These days, I can't help but wonder if there isn't something to it. There's been talk of ghosts around here longer than I can remember. And I've seen a few peculiar things in my time, back when I was young and sprightly enough to hike that fifty mile trail around the lake and camp out."

"What kinds of things?" Ned asked, frankly curious.

"It doesn't matter!" George insisted. "If we fill Bess's head with more ghost stories, none of us will sleep tonight either! Besides, I'm starving. Let's skip the sports store and go home for lunch."

"Hey, none of you looked too happy about that scream we heard again last night," Bess reminded them as they walked back to the car. "Ghosts or no ghosts, something is definitely scary down by the lake at night."

"Like friendly dog-bears," Nancy teased, reaching into George's grocery sack and pulling out a bag of chips.

"That too!" Bess laughed at herself as she took some of the chips and passed the bag to Ned.

Nancy started driving toward the lake. Fifteen minutes later they were well out of town, and George pointed out a shortcut. "Up there," she said, leaning over the backseat. "Make a left, then a quick right. The road's rough, but you get some nice views of the lake. It takes you back to the cottage, and you save about ten minutes."

"This isn't the way we came last night," Nancy said, carefully turning onto the dirt road.

"Too hard to find in the dark, until you know your way. The locals are the only ones who use it. I discovered it hiking last—"

George's words were cut off by Nancy's scream and the squeal of brakes. A pickup truck came hurtling toward her out of a small side road. It was headed straight for Nancy's Mustang.

4

Burgled

Nancy pumped the brakes and gripped the steering wheel. She turned sharply to the right and left, zigzagging to avoid being broadsided by the oncoming truck. She managed to swerve clear, and stop her car on the shoulder of the road.

After doing a complete 360, the pickup truck stalled out inches away from Nancy's Mustang.

Nancy sat numb and stunned. Ned grabbed her hand. "Whew! That was some impressive driving. You okay?"

Nancy felt her heartbeat returning to normal. "I think so," she said, then turned to George and Bess. "How about you guys?"

Bess nodded. Before George could answer, a young man jumped out of the pickup's cab and

33

yelled, "Where did you learn to drive? Can't you read signs?" he added, waving angrily at a sign warning, BLIND SIDE ROAD, TRUCK ENTRANCE.

"Jim?" Bess gasped.

At the sound of his name he looked past Nancy toward the backseat of the convertible.

"If you don't know these roads, you should stay off them!" he shouted.

Ned unsnapped his seat belt and jumped out of the car. He marched up to Jim. "Man, you've got some nerve," Ned said. "You didn't even stop and look before you pulled out."

"So now it's *my* fault?"

Nancy quickly ran between Jim and Ned. She didn't know a thing about Jim, but she wasn't sure Ned realized he had a knife in his belt. Ned was beyond angry, and Jim looked fit to kill. "Bottom line is," she said, her clear blue eyes fixed on Jim, "we're all okay. It could have been a bad accident, but nothing happened. So let it go."

Jim shifted his gaze from Nancy to Ned. He shot one last angry glance at Ned, then heaved a deep sigh. Nancy could almost feel him struggling with his temper. "You've got a point," he finally conceded, though his face was still stony. He turned on his heel and jumped back into the cab of his truck.

As he drove slowly past them, Nancy glimpsed a tarp covering whatever was stowed in the bed of the black pickup. She didn't get much of a look. As soon as he passed Nancy's car, Jim floored the accelerator and raced down the road, trailing a cloud of dust.

Nancy shook her head. "What is that guy's problem?"

"According to what Bess read in the paper, he's got a beef with the whole northern part of the lakeside community," George said. "He's trying to get a coalition of Native American activists to sue the Community Association over setting aside an area of sacred ground."

"Gives him no right to try to run down people who live on this side of the lake!" Ned shot a dark look back down the road as he climbed back into the car.

"He didn't do it on purpose," Nancy and Bess chimed almost in unison. "Besides," Nancy admitted as she gingerly steered back onto the dirt road, "he's right about one thing. I didn't see that sign. I wasn't paying attention."

"He should have stopped, Nan," Ned reminded.

"That too," she agreed. Then she punched the PLAY button on the car's CD player, and Latin dance music blared from the speakers.

A few minutes later they joined the smaller road that ran around the lake shore, and Nancy made a left turn down the long driveway.

"There's Emily!" Bess shouted over the music.

The tall girl was hurrying down the back porch

steps of the cottage. She jogged down the driveway toward them, shouting something, but the music was so loud that Nancy couldn't make out a word. Nancy braked and turned off the car, and the music stopped.

"Did you see him?" Emily gasped, running right up to the convertible and pulling open Nancy's door.

"Who?" Nancy asked. Emily looked pale and scared out of her wits.

"A guy—I think. It was hard to tell. I was heading for the old boathouse when I heard a car pull up. I thought you guys were back, but when I looked, George's van was parked where it is now, and some kind of vehicle was tearing up the drive like it was racing off to a fire."

"A truck?" Ned asked with a frown.

Emily shook her head. "Can't say. Maybe. Maybe an SUV. It was a dark color."

"Jim's truck is black," George murmured.

Emily gripped Nancy's arm, but looked right at George and Bess. "Well, I think you've been burgled."

After a moment of stunned silence, George leaped out of the back of the car. "The cottage has been robbed?"

"George, wait up," Nancy said, running after her. "Don't just rush in there; someone might still be hanging around."

"No one's there," Emily called out. "I just checked.

36

But the door was open, and then there was that vehicle."

"Maybe we should call the cops," Bess suggested. She and Ned joined Nancy on the porch.

Nancy stopped George at the door. "Don't touch anything. If we call the police, they might dust for prints."

Emily let out a low moan. "I already touched the doorknob and checked around inside! I probably disturbed things—but I was only here a minute before you guys pulled up."

"Don't worry. You were just trying to help," Nancy assured her. She walked through the screen door. "When we left for town, did you lock the door?" Nancy asked Bess.

Bess shook her head. "No. We never do. No one breaks into houses around here, at least not during the summer. That's what Jason told us when he gave us the keys. They only lock up if they're going to be gone overnight, and when the season's over."

"Yeah," George added, "and the lock's not a very strong one. The way he put it, if someone wants to break in, no little lock is going to keep them out. But no one's ever broken into this cottage."

"As far as I know, not into my house either," Emily added.

"The place looks pretty okay, doesn't it?" Ned remarked as Nancy flipped on the kitchen light.

"No more messed up than when we left," Nancy noted, taking in the room at a glance. The breakfast dishes were still in the sink, and some plates and glasses were on the table.

"Did you check upstairs?" George asked Emily.

"I didn't have a chance."

"Bess and I will look around up there," George said, running up the wooden staircase.

A loud car horn blared outside from the direction of Emily's house. "Oh! I have to run—I have these guys coming in from town to renovate the old boathouse. Okay if I leave?" She hesitated at the door.

"Sure, there's nothing you can do. And thanks for checking the cottage for us," Nancy said.

Emily went out the door. Through the kitchen window, Nancy watched Emily cross the grass toward the white truck parked in the driveway. It was splattered with mud, and the sign on its side read, NORTH SHORE HAULING, EXCAVATING, AND LANDSCAPING. As Emily approached, two guys jumped out.

Nancy turned her attention back to the countertop. Everything seemed to be in its place: the boom box, the blender, the toaster oven, and the small microwave—the kind of items petty thieves usually love.

"Hey, Nancy, in here!" Ned shouted from the pantry.

Nancy turned from the window and hurried over. "What did you find—" she started to ask, then she noticed the crowbar lying beside a partially pried-up floorboard. "Now, that's weird," she said, crouching down beside Ned. Nancy glanced up at the pantry shelves. The rows of glass Mason jars and canned goods seemed in order. Even the dust on the edges of the shelves seemed undisturbed.

George clattered down the steps and came in through the kitchen. "I heard Ned call you," she said. "Nothing seems to be missing upstairs. Did Ned find something?" she asked, then noticed the floorboard. She let out a low whistle.

"Our burglar was probably in the middle of trying to find something beneath the floorboards here when something made him leave. Maybe he heard Emily outside." Nancy tried to remember what Emily said she had been doing when she heard someone pulling out of the driveway.

"Should we call the cops?" Ned asked, getting up.

"I don't know." Nancy debated with herself a moment. "Nothing's been taken—as far as we can see," Nancy said. She turned to Bess and George. "It *is* weird, though, that he suddenly ran."

"Probably heard our car before we turned down the road," Bess said.

"No way. Just now a truck pulled up at Emily's, and I didn't hear it," Nancy pointed out.

Bess giggled. "True, but that truck wasn't a convertible with the top down and with a CD blaring salsa, Nan. You could have heard us halfway back to Lost Valley."

Nancy laughed. "You've got a point." She looked at the crowbar and the floorboard. "So we're not calling the cops, at least not yet, so I won't worry about fingerprints. I really want to see if something *is* beneath this board, though." She shot a questioning look toward George. "Okay if I finish what the mystery man started?"

"Be my guest," George said and shrugged. "I think next summer Jen and Jay are going to redo the whole kitchen and pantry. Besides, we can nail it back down."

Nancy worked the crowbar carefully around the old plank. It came off fairly easily. She pulled out the small penlight she kept on her key chain, and aimed the narrow beam at the crevice. All she saw was the usual old house debris: a thick layer of dirt, bits of paper that had slipped between cracks in the floor over the years, dustballs, ancient peanut shells left by a mouse, and the remains of a mouse nest. She felt vaguely disappointed. "At least we know the burglar wouldn't have found much of value here," Nancy said.

"I'll go get a hammer and some nails, so we can put this back," George volunteered.

"Great," Nancy said, starting to get up. Suddenly,

she noticed something glinting in a patch of sunlight that was streaming through the open pantry door. She knelt down and let out a low laugh. "Now *this* is interesting."

Ned dropped down beside her and looked at the floor. "New nails on several boards. Which means—"

Nancy finished Ned's sentence, "Today's not the first time someone's been here looking for something."

"I don't believe it. You mean the whole time we've been here someone's been systematically burgling our house!" Bess cried in dismay.

"Maybe, or maybe earlier. You guys have only been here most of August. Could have happened last winter, or in the spring when Jen and Jason are only around on weekends."

Nancy's words calmed Bess down some. She added, "Look, Bess, whoever was skulking around today probably won't be back for a long time. They almost got caught in the act." Nancy stood up and stretched. "I'm going to see if Emily's finished talking to those workmen. I want to see where she was when she heard the vehicle pull out of this driveway. I can't believe we didn't run into anyone on our way in."

"Except Jim," Ned reminded her.

Nancy frowned. "Right. Jim." She thought about

Jim a moment and made a mental note to find out if that road he pulled out of circled back in this direction. Still, it was hard to believe he rushed out of the house in time to have almost run into them. With a shake of her head she said, "We drove another five minutes or so before we got here. Emily seemed to think we should have seen someone pulling out of the drive."

"She didn't exactly say that," Ned pointed out. "She wondered if we saw someone on the way in. That could have meant on our way in from the main road."

"True," Nancy conceded. "I'll go ask her now. But in the meantime, maybe you guys should check things out a little more thoroughly. The burglar seemed interested in something beneath the floorboard, but he could have made off with some jewelry or something small we wouldn't notice right away."

"Maybe it was a homeless person who wandered in," Bess suggested. "Maybe someone hungry."

George opened the refrigerator and peered inside. "But none of the food seems to have been touched," she said.

"No, and I don't think whoever was here came to steal something easy to grab," Nancy said. "Whoever it was expected to find something tucked away in this house."

Outside, shielding her eyes from the sun, Nancy looked over at Emily's driveway. The truck was still parked, but Emily and the two men were nowhere in sight. Nancy made her way down the hill toward the boathouse. Its stone and wood exterior matched both the main house and the Fayne's cottage. As she walked past the garden shed, she heard Emily's voice:

"Time's running out, guys. . . ."

Nancy looked around the corner of the shed.

Emily was standing there talking urgently to the two workmen. As Nancy approached, both men looked up, startled. "Just a sec," Emily said, handing the bigger man some cash.

"I can come back later," Nancy said, turning to leave.

"No—Kevin and Dale here were just leaving."

"You bet!" the bigger man said, pocketing the cash. He mumbled something to Emily, then motioned for the other man to get in the truck.

"See you tomorrow," he called out the passenger window. He backed the truck into the turnaround, and drove up the long gravel drive.

"Sorry to bother you," Nancy said, looking around the lawn. The boathouse and shed were definitely in need of repair: broken shingles on the roof, cracked windowpanes, and a door half off its hinges—bravely secured with a shiny new padlock.

"No bother at all." Emily smiled as she watched Nancy take a look around. "I know. This place really

43

is a mess," she said with a sigh. "More than I bargained for when I took it on!"

"Bess said you bought it only a few months ago."

Emily nodded. "I had my heart set on the place." A determined expression came across her face. "And I'm going to make it work, even if I go broke doing it!"

Nancy put her hand on Emily's arm. "My dad always says that if you believe enough in your dreams, they do come true—with a little work."

"More like a *lot* of work and even more money!" Emily joked.

"I wonder, did those guys see anyone on their way here?" Nancy asked.

Emily shook her head. "I asked. They said there was a truck on one of the back roads a little earlier driving fast, but they didn't say when exactly. They do lots of hauling and landscaping jobs on this end of the lake."

"Right. I have another question. It's about the cottage. It used to be part of your property, right?"

"*My* property?" Emily pursed her lips. "Never. I mean it was parceled off and sold ages ago, like in the nineteen-forties or fifties. It hasn't been part of the big house acreage for years. I wish it were, though," she said. "Of course, that would have made this place even less affordable!"

A wistful note in her voice piqued Nancy's curiosity, but before she could ask her more, she heard the crunch of gravel on the driveway. She turned to see a candy-apple red Volkswagen Beetle stopping in the turnaround. At the sight of the car, Emily's face paled. As the door opened, she gasped. "How in the world did *you* find me here?"

5

The Uninvited Guest

The driver climbed out of the car and spoke in a hurt voice. "Like, maybe you could look a little bit happier to see me!" He held his thumb and index finger about an inch apart. He wore a bright yellow oversized T-shirt with a pair of long, baggy khaki shorts. He was very handsome.

Emily bit her lip and blushed. "Oh, Ravi, I'm sorry. I'm just so busy, I haven't had time for company."

Ravi looked at Nancy, and his eyebrows shot up.

"I'm not company!" Nancy said very quickly. "I'm staying with my friends at the cottage next door." She started to back away. Emily was definitely not pleased to see her friend, and Nancy thought maybe she should make herself scarce.

"You don't have to leave," Emily told Nancy, then

walked up to Ravi and gave him a quick peck on the cheek. "Sorry, Ravi, I didn't mean to sound so impolite. But I thought you were in New York, in film school. What are you doing here? How in the world did you find me?"

Ravi's smile broadened. "Don't you remember I was your main competition in our investigative journalism class back at the U? I'm a good detective. Anyway, my classes ended in mid-July, and since then I've been working on my master's project. Remember?"

"Not exactly," Emily admitted, looking uncomfortable.

Ravi rolled his eyes. "I only used to talk about it all the time when we were undergrads. I'm doing a documentary on lost lands, communities flooded out by government hydroelectric projects in the early and midtwentieth century. Moonlight Lake wasn't far from New York, plus it fit the bill. Then when I checked the alumni Web site I found out you'd bought a place on this very lake and—it was like fate was pointing me here." He shoved his hands in the pockets of his shorts and looked around. "Pretty impressive spread, Emily. Don't know how you managed it."

"Family money," she said curtly.

"Look," he said, sounding apologetic. "Your phone was unlisted, so I couldn't call ahead, but if you want me to leave—"

"Nan!"

At the sound of Ned's voice, Nancy turned, relieved to see him heading in her direction. Whatever was going on between Ravi and Emily, Nancy felt it was private. She grinned as Ned walked up. He had changed into baggy swim trunks and was rubbing sunblock on his arms. "Game for a swim?" he asked, then greeted Ravi with a smile. "Hi, I'm Ned Nickerson."

"Ravi. Ravi Bindrath."

Emily clapped her hand to her forehead. "Sorry. I forgot about introductions. This is Nancy Drew. Like she said, she's staying with friends in that cottage over there."

Ravi looked over at the cottage. "Matches this place. Bet it was a guest house back when this place was built—when was that, Em? Nineteen-twenty or so?"

"Uh, something like that," she said. "But look, since you're here, you might as well crash here tonight," she added, putting her hand on Ravi's arm. "You just surprised me, and I have been awfully busy with renovations, repairs, and then some freelance work to keep me afloat."

"I promise I won't overstay my welcome. Like I said, I'm actually on a research mission. I just wanted to drop by since you're in the neighborhood."

"It will be nice to have company for a change," Emily said. "I've been keeping to myself too much.

48

My neighbor Bess was lecturing me about that earlier today," she admitted with a smile. "Why don't you guys bring Bess and George over after dinner, and we'll all watch a movie together?"

Ravi lit up. "And I know the perfect film. I'll go back out to town later and rent it!"

"Great," Nancy said. "Meanwhile, that lake looks pretty inviting." She turned to Ned. "A swim sounds perfect. I'll go change."

Nancy started for the house, Ned close behind. "Are Bess and George coming along?" she asked.

Ned shook his head. "Bess is tackling the laundry, and George didn't want to leave her alone at the house. Bess is still spooked about the break-in."

They had almost reached the property line when Ravi shouted across the lawn. "Hey, guys, watch out for the weather," he warned. "The radio's predicting strong storms this afternoon and tonight."

"Thanks for the heads-up," Ned said.

A few minutes later Ned and Nancy stood on the weathered planks of the lakeside dock behind the cottage. "How about swimming out to that platform?" Ned asked.

Nancy looked out over the lake. The floating platform was situated about a third of the way between the shore and the hilly island that George had mentioned rowing over to see some sunset. She grinned. "You bet. We can keep an eye on the weather while we catch our breath." Eyes dancing, she challenged Ned to a race to the platform. "Race you!"

"Ha! As if you have a chance to win!" he scoffed. "On the count of three!" he said, putting down the sunblock. Nancy kicked off her flip-flops. "One. Two. Three!"

Nancy dove headfirst off the dock and swam strongly underwater for several yards before she surfaced and broke into a freestyle. She could see Ned out of the corner of her eye. It was a close race.

Nancy kicked hard and took long, smooth strokes. She felt herself gaining speed as she cut through the water. She gave one last powerful kick and managed to lay one hand on the platform a heartbeat before Ned. "Beat ya!" She laughed, hoisting herself out of the water.

"By an inch." Ned huffed, climbing out as well.

"Doesn't matter by how much," Nancy pointed out, and sat down on the wood boards. The platform was pleasantly warm from having baked beneath the sun all day. Sunlight streamed across Nancy's back.

Ned settled down next to her. For a moment they simply soaked in the view. The sky and water were blue, though the weather had grown a bit humid, and there was haze on the horizon. Flat-bottomed tour boats cruised in the distance. White, yellow, and blue sails decorated the sailboats lazily skimming the surface of the water in the mildest of breezes.

From their vantage point Nancy got her first over-all view of Moonlight Lake's north shore. A surpris-ingly thick remnant of old forest lay to the right of the cottage, curving with the shoreline. Nancy shielded her eyes, and through the trees she caught a glimpse of a rather large dock. It gleamed in the light and looked new. "Must be the Lawrence-Joneses' place," Nancy told Ned, pointing across the glitter-ing water.

"And that must be Steve Delmonico's camp," Ned said as he gestured toward a beach that lay to the right of Emily's property. Empty rowboats bobbed on the blue water next to a fleet of canoes. The dock was sizeable, and from the platform it looked to be in good repair.

Nancy nodded. She could understand why Camp Moonlight's owner was ticked off by Emily acquiring the old Malone property. She didn't know where the property line was, but it seemed like Emily's pur-chase abutted his camp—effectively cutting off any possibility of expanding Camp Moonlight's facilities. Nancy couldn't quite tell what lay on the other side of the camp's beachfront. The shore jutted out into a rocky promontory, with a thin strand of stunted pines obscuring the view of whatever lay beyond.

"Camp looks pretty deserted," Ned observed. "Guess all the kids are gone."

"Bess told me that only the maintenance staff and

administration is around this week. By next weekend they'll probably have stowed all those boats. Looks lonely without the campers," Nancy said, leaning back on her elbows.

"Delmonico, the camp owner, came off as a pretty nasty piece of work," Ned commented.

"Well, George and Bess's neighbors, the Lawrence-Joneses, were not exactly pleasant either," Nancy said, remembering the incidents of the previous evening.

"What do you think about that attempted burglary this afternoon?" Ned asked.

"Hard to say," Nancy remarked slowly. "With so much small stuff in sight that would be easy to grab, why would someone pry up a floorboard?"

"Like you said earlier, they were probably looking for something in particular."

Nancy nodded. She rolled over on her stomach and propped her chin in her hands. "So far, that's the only explanation."

"You did hear someone snooping around outside last night," Ned reminded her. "Maybe they were casing the joint."

"While we were there? I doubt it. Unless, of course, someone is just trying to spook Bess and George."

Ned threw back his head and laughed. "Bess was born spooked! But it would take more than a prowler to unnerve George Fayne."

"Emily didn't really see the car that pulled away. . . ," Nancy recalled.

"Or *truck*!" Ned added pointedly. "I know Bess *wants* that Jim guy to be some kind of dream man, but he seems like a pretty unsavory character to me."

"He's not *that* bad," Nancy said. "Then again, if I could figure out why someone interested in Native American rights would be prying up a floorboard in a house and trying to burgle something, Jim would top my list of suspects." Nancy thought a minute. "I don't know how he could have been at the cottage and then run into us when he did."

"He knows the back roads. Even driving them slowly, it took us only five minutes or so to get back to the house after we ran into him. So who else is on the list?"

Nancy sighed. "It's a *very* short list. There's no one else on it yet!" With that, she pillowed her head on her arms, and closed her eyes. She pictured the pantry and the pried-up board and reminded herself to confirm that Bess had left the door open and that no one had jimmied the back door lock. "We have to watch the weather," she mumbled as she began to drift into a nap.

It seemed a second later that Ned was shaking her. "Nancy, wake up!"

Even before she opened her eyes, she felt the platform rocking in the water. Nancy sat up quickly and saw clouds mounting on the northwest horizon. They were tall, dark, and menacing. As she rubbed the sleep from her eyes, she heard a clap of thunder. It was still far off, but the wind was picking up.

"We'd better get out of here, now!" she said.

Ned shook his head. "I can't believe we both drifted off like that. I have no idea what time it is."

"We'll figure that out later," Nancy said. With that, they both jumped into the lake and started swimming toward the shore.

But the water was much rougher than it had been before, and waves surged above Nancy's head. She felt as if she were swimming against a current. Though she aimed herself toward the cottage's dock, she found herself being pulled back toward the platform. She felt like she was swimming in slow motion. The water was slapping her face. Nancy gritted her teeth. She was a powerful swimmer. Doubling her effort, she began to make some headway.

"We're not making much progress!" Ned gasped. He was a short distance away from her, and she could see that he, too, was struggling.

"It's getting worse!" she yelled over the raging wind. "Let's head for Camp Moonlight's dock. We've drifted over too far to get back to the cottage. We can wait at the camp until the storm passes," she shouted over the wind.

Ned yelled something back. But over the wail of

the wind she couldn't make out his words. He lifted his arm and pointed toward Camp Moonlight.

Good, he heard me! she thought as she managed to change direction. Though they were still swimming into the wind, the shore seemed closer.

She glanced over at Ned and panic clenched her chest. She had lost sight of him. A gust of wind sent a spray of water into her eyes. "Ned!" she screamed. She spotted him struggling a few yards ahead of her. He was battling the rough water, but gaining on Camp Moonlight's beachfront. Phew!

The waves were getting high, and now the first drops of rain spattered the lake's surface. The wind's howl grew piercing, and Nancy noticed the dark gray clouds tinged with a frightening but familiar greenish hue. Do they have tornadoes in this part of the country? she wondered. But she forced back the thought and summoned another burst of strength.

Ned reached the dock first. He located a ladder and quickly scrambled up to the pier. Nancy soon followed. Lightning flashed in the sky, and thunder crashed too close for comfort.

"Hurry, Nancy! We've got to get shelter!" he shouted.

Nancy's fingers closed around Ned's and she struggled up the slippery steps. "We made it!" she gasped, the force of the gale practically knocking her off her feet. The words had barely crossed her lips when she felt a strong tingling sensation in the air.

"Get down!" she shouted, hitting the deck and pulling Ned down with her. She flattened herself on the wood surface and prayed lightning wouldn't strike them. Then thunder clapped, deafening Nancy. An explosive crack followed, shaking the dock.

Nancy's head jerked up in time to witness one of the beech trees near the pier split in two—and half of the tree began crashing down toward Ned and Nancy!

6

A Killer Storm

Just before the tree crashed down, Ned pushed Nancy off the dock and onto the sand. The dock creaked and groaned under the tree trunk's weight. A second later, the edge of the dock broke off.

"That was awfully close!" Nancy gasped. She lifted her head. Through torrents of rain she could see the sky to the north was already brighter. The fast-moving storm was flying out over the lake. Nancy's heart rate slowed, and she scrambled to her feet. She let the rain wash some of the sand off her shoulders.

"We'd better seek shelter here in the camp," Ned suggested.

"Hey, here comes Steve now!" Nancy pointed across the beach. The camp director was barreling toward them.

"Yeah, and there's Tiny!" Ned groaned. The dog was soaked from the rain and barking furiously. But at the sight of Nancy, Tiny's tail began to wag. "At least he's friendly."

Steve was shouting something Nancy couldn't quite hear over the wind. Finally, when he was just within earshot one word reached her: "*trespassing*"!

For a moment Nancy was rendered speechless.

Ned charged right up to Steve. "*Trespassing*? Have you lost it or what?! This storm is serious. We should all get inside somewhere till it blows over."

"Get out of here now!" Steve fumed. He was the same height as Ned, but outweighed him by at least a third.

"Ned." Nancy stepped up, and grabbed his arm. "Let's go."

Ned huffed, but didn't balk at Nancy's suggestion. She steered him toward a path leading into the woods that fringed the beach near the camp.

"Not that way!" Steve planted himself directly in her way, barring her from the path. He moved surprisingly quickly for a big man. Still clutching Tiny's collar, he said, "That's *my* land at least for a good half acre, and you are not welcome on my land. No one connected with that Malone property is. Go back the way you came." He jerked his head toward the water. "I don't tolerate trespassers, *period.*"

Nancy's blood began to boil.

Trespassing! Nancy was incredulous. "There's a dangerous storm over the lake, and you want us to *swim* back to our place?"

"I don't care *what's* going on. So get out of here now, or I'll set Tiny on you!"

Nancy tried not to laugh, but then looked at the dog. Apparently Steve's anger had the animal agitated. Besides, they *were* on the dog's territory.

Ned glared at Steve, but Nancy caught his arm. "Don't bother with him." Without a backward glance at Steve, she declared coolly, "We're going through the woods. I don't care *whose* woods these are. But I'm not getting back into that water."

She walked right around Steve, trying not to wince as the sand gave way to a narrow trail.

"You'll regret this!" he railed after them.

Nancy paid him no mind. She kept marching with as much dignity as she could muster. When they reached a bend in the path, she sagged against Ned. "I forgot I had no shoes!" she admitted, rubbing her feet.

"Tell me about it," Ned moaned. "But look at it this way—at least the rain is lighter here."

"And the thunder's pretty far off now," Nancy noticed. "At least we don't have to try to *run* barefoot through the woods." She paused at a trail marker. Arrows in various colors were painted on its side. Nancy's instinct was to go straight, but the path

59

stopped at the marker, branching off to the right and the left. A tangle of rhododendron bushes would have made abandoning the path a challenge—even if Nancy and Ned were wearing shoes.

She checked out the trails. The one to the right led back down to the lake, through what looked to be very scrubby, thorny bushes. The trail on the left climbed up the side of the hill, where a low cliff of black rock glistened through the trees. The forest looked deeper here, but the path had less underbrush and was covered with soft pine needles. Nancy figured that campers or staff maintained the trails. "I guess we go this way!"

"We could hit Emily's by going up a bit, then cutting over," Ned suggested.

Nancy made a face. "Can't say I love the idea. She and Ravi seem to have something to work out, so I'd rather not run into them again. But you're right. Let's stick to the path here awhile then cut over. As the trees get bigger there's less undergrowth, so the going will be easier even without a path."

As they proceeded down the trail, sunlight filtered through the trees, making steam rise from the recently soaked forest floor. Birds sang high overhead, and the leaves were dripping. As she gingerly made her way, Nancy tried to focus on how pretty the forest looked and smelled after a rain, and to forget about her poor feet.

Up ahead a branch creaked. Nancy froze. "Did you hear that?" she whispered, curious to see what kind of wildlife was rummaging in the brush.

Ned nodded.

"Think it's a deer?" she whispered again. She took a few cautious steps forward.

"Too quiet to be Tiny or Steve!" Ned joked.

Nancy laughed silently and walked as quietly as she could a little farther up the path. Through the leaves of the trees, she glimpsed something dark crouching down in front of the face of the cliff. It didn't look like a deer.

"What are you doing here?" Ned's voice behind her made the crouching figure jump up.

"Jim?" Nancy couldn't quite believe her eyes. Then she looked from him to the base of the cliff. At first she didn't notice the shallow cave. A low cairn of rocks was arranged at the mouth of the cave. Jim was holding something in his hand, but Nancy couldn't quite make out what.

As soon as he saw Ned and Nancy he tossed what he was holding back into the cave and shielded the entrance with his body. "Are you clones, or what?"

Ned shook his head. "It seems *you're* the one turning up everywhere today. This is private property."

"Delmonico doesn't care if I hike in here. Anyway, what he doesn't know won't bother him. What's your excuse?" Jim challenged Ned.

Nancy touched Ned's arm. "Look," she whispered, "whatever Jim's up to is his business. If he's looking for a run-in with Delmonico, that's his problem. Let's just get out of here."

Nancy was grateful when Ned agreed readily. "Right. Besides, this is where we should cut off to get back to the house. Otherwise, we'd have to tackle the dirt road barefoot too."

Bess greeted them a little while later from the yard. "You guys are a sight for sore eyes, even if you do look about as bad as my laundry!" She and George were taking a load of soaking wet laundry off the line and throwing it in a basket. Ned and Nancy had stopped to retrieve their flip-flops from the deck.

"Tell me about it," Nancy said, turning on the garden hose to wash off her feet. They were sore and filthy. Ned stuck out his feet for her to hose down too.

"I was getting worried when the storm came in and you weren't back here yet. But I figured you guys would take shelter somewhere," George said.

Ned and Nancy exchanged a look. "Not exactly!" they said in unison, then began to laugh.

"Actually, it's a long story, and I'll fill you in on the details later," Nancy said. "First, I'm hitting the shower."

Then Nancy remembered Bess had told her the night before that the cottage didn't have a dryer—

and all those wet clothes! "Do you want to run in to town to a laundromat? I'll drive you in before dinner, and we can pick up pizza or something."

"No need," George answered. "Since we're going to Emily's to watch a video tonight, I'm pretty sure she'll let us use her dryer. I'll call to check."

"I'm curious to see what movie Ravi picked out for the occasion!" Bess remarked.

A couple of hours later, to her dismay, Bess found out. "What a guy flick!" she grumbled from an overstuffed chair in Emily's sprawling living room.

Ned and Nancy were curled up together on one of the two couches in the room. George was sprawled on the floor in front of the TV. The other couch held Ravi and Emily—with a good three feet and a bowl of popcorn between them. Nancy had been trying to figure out their relationship all night. Had they dated in college, or were they just friends?

But at the moment her eyes were riveted on the oversized TV. The movie was a top-notch Prohibition era mystery she'd never seen before, *Dark Waters Run Red*.

"It's not a guy flick," George corrected Bess. "It's just film noir. A real classic."

"Shhh!" Ravi commanded from the couch. Nancy turned and saw he was perched at the edge of his seat, eyes bright and excited as he viewed the screen.

She quickly turned back in time to see the action. Heavily armed government agents surrounded a gangster's house. Roaring Twenties dance music blared from the house's open windows out onto the driveway. Barely visible on the dimly lit screen were the shiny black sedans parked outside the house. The female lead, a gangster's moll, dressed in a sparkly flapper outfit, strolled onto the porch, a long cigarette holder propped between her fingers. The camera zoomed in on her face. She stared with a bored expression beyond the porch out into the night. Suddenly, her face registered pure panic.

She screamed and bolted back into the house. "Guys," she cried in a pure Brooklyn accent, "we've been busted!"

With that, pandemonium broke loose, and a shoot-out lit up the screen. The camera panned back and Nancy gasped.

"Why, that looks just like the Malone house!"

Ravi whooped with glee. "Because it is! And because once upon a time this place was the real hideaway of notorious mobster, Mike Malone!"

7

A Secret Revealed

Emily jumped up. She stared down at Ravi, who was still on the sofa. "Is this some kind of sick joke?"

Ravi seemed stunned by Emily's reaction. He stood up slowly. "Emily, I can't believe you, of all people, didn't know the history of this place before you bought it. I thought it was beyond cool, considering your work."

"What work, and what makes you think this place is an old gangster hideout?" Nancy asked. George grabbed the remote and stopped the tape. "Wasn't it probably just rented out for some location shooting?"

"Of course it was rented by the movie company, long after Mike Malone was carted off to jail. In fact, the film was made long after the valley was flooded—which is how I found out about this. I was researching the lost lands in the area, and a footnote in one of my references mentioned how when they filmed this movie in the forties, they had to avoid shots that showed the full expanse of the lake. Back in Malone's day, there actually was a small lake here. It was big enough to swim in, I guess, and it was secluded. Made a good place to hang low after some caper."

"I can't believe this," Emily moaned, sinking back down on the couch. "All I knew is this place was called the old Malone place. I didn't know Mike Malone had anything to do with it."

Ravi shook his head in disbelief. "Emily, you've been working on a documentary on Prohibition era gangsters for what—two, three years now?"

"You have?" Nancy was impressed. Her own interest in solving crimes had made a bit of a hobby out of learning about the exploits of the G-men and how they battled the brazen Chicago mob. At home she even had a WANTED poster of Al Capone.

"Whenever I have time," Emily said dully. "It's a long-term project. I do some, then I wait to get more money together to film and research some more."

Ravi looked incredulous. "I can't believe this woman." He turned to Nancy. "Emily's outline for this project, and the first taped segments, were part of her senior thesis. It's what won her a position as a stringer for the news channel." Addressing Emily again, he continued. "I don't know why you're being so modest about it. But so what if it's a long term project? How could you not know about Mike Malone and his connection to this area?"

"I was concentrating on Chicago-area people like Capone. I hadn't hit the East Coast, New York–Boston mobs yet," Emily said defensively.

"What's the problem?" Ned asked. "I think it makes the whole place more interesting. Hey, if this was really some Prohibition era goon's getaway, maybe there's loot stashed somewhere."

"Like stolen jewels?" Bess said, suddenly interested.

Ned cracked up. "I was just joking, Bess."

"Believe me, back in the twenties when this guy was busted," Ravi said, "the Feds would have scoured every inch of this place."

Nancy nodded agreement. "They'd have been looking for more than jewels and stolen property back then. The G-men would have carted off all the weapons, booze, and the like. It's been years, and this house has surely had several owners since Malone." She questioned Emily with a glance.

"I imagine so," Emily said tightly. "The family I bought it from had it since the fifties."

"But," George mused, "maybe someone else thinks like Bess. Maybe that's why someone tried burgling us today."

Bess turned to Emily. "That's why you're upset, isn't it? It's hard to live in a place where someone's been murdered!" Bess shuddered. "Or maybe it's the ghosts of Malone's victims that have been haunting us over the past week!"

"Or Malone himself!" Ravi said in a deep spooky voice, then broke into a laugh.

"Don't joke about things like that. You don't know what you're talking about," Bess said, offended.

"Enough about ghosts, robbers, loot, and Mike Malone!" Nancy declared, getting up. It was obvious Bess was getting carried away with things, and Emily looked really upset. "It's getting late. Let's grab the laundry from the dryer and head back home," she suggested.

"Good idea," George said. The girls waved good-bye to Emily and Ravi, and headed into the mud-room that ran along the back of the house where the washer and dryer were hooked up.

A few minutes later they were carrying the laundry baskets across the lawn by the beam of Ned's flashlight.

"More storms coming," George noted, gesturing out over the lake. Sheet-lightning illuminated the sky, but the storm was too far off to hear the thunder.

"Or blowing past us," Nancy said, realizing the temperature had dropped a bit. She put down her basket to zip up her pale blue hooded sweatshirt, when she caught the movement of something out of the corner of her eye. She was sure she saw a dim light bobbing through the woods between the Fayne cottage and the Lawrence-Joneses' place. It flickered again for a moment, then was gone.

Nancy decided not to mention what she'd seen to the others; she didn't want to scare them. She picked up her basket, but as they approached the cottage, she handed it to Ned. "Ned, I've got to get something from the car. I might hang out here a few minutes."

"Want me along?" Ned said.

Nancy shook her head. "I'll only be a few minutes, then I'll be back. Bess'll feel safer from ghosts or whatever with you in the house."

Ned pecked Nancy on the cheek and headed inside. Nancy went to her car. She popped open the glove compartment and took out a flashlight. She made her way through the brush into the forest.

She stopped for a moment and tried to get her bearings. The light she saw had bobbed off to her left and deeper into the forest. Moving as quietly as she could, she aimed her flashlight down at the ground, not wanting to betray her presence to whomever was lurking nearby.

Though Nancy had downplayed Bess's fears earlier, she was beginning to suspect Bess was right. Someone was "haunting" the Malone property. Just not a ghost. Someone alive, curious, and on a personal treasure hunt for something he or she believed Malone had stashed away on his property before he was carted off to jail.

George's suggestion that there might still be loot around had seemed pretty ludicrous. But Nancy was beginning to wonder. Still, she thought, why root around in the cottage, when the Malone house itself would have certainly made a better hiding place? For all Nancy knew, the cottage might have been built after Malone had gone to jail. She made a mental note to ask Emily if all the buildings on the original property dated from the same era.

Nancy also planned to ask if Emily had been the victim of any weird incidents—either burglaries or any kind of harassment. Come to think of it, Steve Delmonico seemed more than capable of trying to either spook Emily into selling her land, or just make her life miserable.

And then there was Jim. Nancy had almost forgotten about him. He had been doing something strange in Steve's woods today. Definitely something he didn't want Nancy and Ned to see. Was he digging around looking for something? He was intimate with the land around here, and was probably well-acquainted with local legend. Finding unclaimed money or jewelry would be a boon to someone embroiled in legal actions over tribal rights.

Suddenly a shrill screech pierced through the trees. Nancy froze. That same scream again. It had come from just ahead of her. It came from the same direction where she'd last seen that light.

Someone. Some *woman* was in trouble big-time. Nancy sprang into action. Sticking to the trail she had found, she broke into a slow, careful jog. Branches scraped her cheek.

She crashed through the brush, not caring who heard her. Suddenly, something caught her ankle. A blinding flash of light shone through the woods. Unable to see, Nancy lost her balance and flew face down into a tangle of thorny berry bushes.

8

Blinded by the Light

For a moment, Nancy lay in the bramble, stunned. Then, with a low moan, she gingerly freed herself of the thorny branches and got back on her feet. Her eyes were still having trouble regaining any night vision.

Though her arms and legs felt bruised and sore, she knew she wasn't hurt. She touched her face hoping she hadn't scratched herself up too badly. Apparently, when she'd tripped, she'd broken her fall with her arms before hitting the ground.

Tripped! One minute Nancy was running, the next she ran straight into something. *But what?* And what was that light? Nancy wondered, looking around. Gradually, the world around her came into focus.

She spotted her flashlight lying in the middle of the path—right next to a wire. With sudden insight, Nancy realized what must have happened. The wire had been connected to some sort of camera flash. This camera setup probably belonged to naturalists. "I really blew it this time," she groaned softly.

The wire had broken, but by grabbing one end, Nancy followed it back to where it had been tied around a tree. A little farther down the trail she saw a small animal carcass dangling from a branch. Nancy recoiled in distaste. It was really gross. Obviously, it was some sort of bait—this time, tied up out of easy reach of Tiny, or any other passing dog.

Nancy couldn't believe her bad luck. As she had run through the woods, she had stumbled across what was surely one of the Lawrence-Joneses' research setups. Nancy wasn't sure what to do. Whoever had screamed hadn't screamed again—just like the other night. But was the person all right? Nancy guessed she'd probably made enough noise by setting off the flash and crashing into the brush that any wrongdoer would be long gone.

Meanwhile Nancy's conscience was pricking her. She had managed to mess up some of the Lawrence-Joneses' work. They would be on Bess and George's case for sure now, and probably raise trouble when Jen and Jason got home.

Suddenly she heard voices coming toward her. Before Nancy could think about it, she ducked behind a boulder and peered around the edge.

"We're in luck this time!"

The sound of Millicent Lawrence-Jones's voice made Nancy cringe. A moment later a bright flashlight beam illuminated the path. Nancy tried to work up her nerve to show herself to the couple. But before she had a chance, Caspar dropped to his knees and let out an angry exclamation.

"Caspar, what's wrong?"

"One of those kids tripped the wire—this is a sneaker mark! Either it was that mysterious prowler we've glimpsed before, or it was that crew from next door horsing around in the woods. Well, we'll get a good picture of whomever it was, that's for sure."

"So we missed the screech owl again!" Millicent said.

Screech owl! Nancy's jaw dropped. She'd never heard one before, but she knew from reading that they had an eerie sound that Native Americans often associated with death and the spirit world. Nancy felt both relieved and rather foolish. So it wasn't a woman in danger or one of Bess's ghosts. At least that'll put Bess's mind at rest, she thought.

"I might as well reset the camera now," Caspar grumbled. "But really, our research here is becoming pretty impossible—between those kids in the house and that canoe out on the lake at night. If our moon-light boater doesn't cool it soon, he'll spook all the Canada geese away from the inlet beyond the camp. If that *other* noise doesn't drive them off first."

What noise? Nancy wondered.

"It's as if someone's digging a well somewhere," Millicent said. "But why at night? And who?"

"I don't know, but I'm getting sick of it all. This lake's getting overdeveloped, and newcomers have no respect for the wildlife here. Believe me, next year I bet those geese don't stop here."

"That would be awful, Caspar," Millicent said, stooping down to help him reset the wire. "It's a major layover on their migration route."

"Yeah, well, these kids don't care. I thought they'd be gone by now—at least those campers have left for the season. But now there are more kids and more trouble. Nothing I've tried so far has worked. I think the time's come to stop being nice."

Nancy couldn't believe her ears. Were these people fanatics or what? It was one thing to tell off a neighbor who was annoying you. It was quite an-other to plot to scare them. Nancy was tempted to march right up to Caspar and say whatever he was planning—or what he had already done—bordered on serious harassment.

But Nancy forced herself to calm down. These people were angry, and she didn't want to confront them alone in the woods. She'd make a point of visiting them tomorrow and telling them off. She probably still owed them an explanation for tonight, but they also owed George and Bess some sort of apology for spooking them half to death.

She waited until they finished setting up their camera. As soon as they left, she walked quietly back to the cottage, arriving in the backyard just as another thunderstorm broke.

She raced up the porch steps, and the back door flew open in her face. It was Ned, looking worried. "You're okay!" he exclaimed, then shouted over his shoulder, "You don't have to call the cops."

"The cops?" Nancy hurried into the house after Ned. George was just hanging up the phone and Bess looked petrified.

"Oh, Nan," Bess cried, relief washing over her face. "You went to the car and then seemed to be gone a long time, and then there was that scream!"

"We went out looking for you, but just as we started into the woods, Bess thought she saw someone sneaking around the side of the house. We ran back here," George said. "But we couldn't see anything."

"I thought, maybe it was time to call the state police," Ned added.

"Oh, I'm so sorry I freaked you guys out," Nancy said with a sigh. Of course they worried something had happened to her. After all, hadn't she herself believed someone was in trouble in the woods? "At least you'll be happy to know it wasn't one of your ghosts, Bess."

"Then what?" Ned asked. Then he seemed to take a good look at Nancy for the first time. "What happened to you anyway? You look like you took quite a fall."

Nancy looked down at her jeans. They were muddy, and her favorite blue sweatshirt was caked with dirt and leaves. Shallow scratches marred the back of her hands.

"Yeah, well, thanks to the Lawrence-Joneses, I managed to trip and fall into a bramble bush," Nancy said, looking in the cabinets for something to put on her cuts. The more she thought about what happened in the woods, the angrier she got.

"Here, I'll get it," George said, ducking into the pantry. A moment later she came back with some antiseptic spray and a couple of bandages.

While Nancy washed her hands at the sink, she told her story. "Those awful screams are apparently the call of a screech owl!" she said. "Not half as romantic as ghosts of drowned valley children, or Malone's murder victims. Although the Lawrence-Joneses *are* hopping mad. They figured it was one of us who set off the flash."

George, Bess, and Ned looked quizzical.

77

Nancy laughed. "My sneaker prints. It's very muddy, and I certainly made a big mess back there."

"If it's a screech owl," Bess said, sinking down in a chair, "no one was getting hurt—except you!"

"Nothing serious," Nancy said, deciding then and there to keep Caspar's comments to herself. She wanted to talk to him herself. Besides, with little sleep the night before, the frantic swim this afternoon, and her encounter in the woods, Nancy was exhausted.

"Look, guys, can we talk more about this in the morning? I'm about ready to fall asleep on my feet," she said, barely able to stifle a yawn.

After a quick shower, Nancy crawled into bed with the vague feeling that she had forgotten to ask Bess and George about something. But the minute her head hit the pillow, she dropped into a deep and dreamless sleep.

It seemed just seconds later that Nancy's eyes popped open. Her lids were heavy, and for a moment she couldn't remember where she was. Then she heard the sound of something being moved in the attic above her room.

But there is no attic! Nancy thought. George told her that when Bess was complaining about ghosts. Nancy sat bolt upright in bed and looked at her clock. It was past three A.M. She'd been asleep for at least four hours.

Swinging her legs out of bed, she threw her robe over her pajamas. Quietly, she stood up and listened. Except for the distant hum of the refrigerator cycling on downstairs, and the whirr of a fan coming in from George and Bess's room, the house seemed totally silent.

Maybe she'd been dreaming? Or maybe it was just mice in the rafters. But then she heard the noise again. Something sliding across the floor above her head. No mouse ever made that much noise. George had to be wrong. There had to be another level to this house—maybe a crawl space.

Nancy grabbed a bedside flashlight, then opened the door to her room to investigate. Maybe there was a small trap door at the end of the hall, or in the ceiling. She walked past the closed door to George and Bess's room, and then past Ned's. The hall was short and ended at the bathroom, which was off to the right. She ran the beam of the flashlight around the wall and the ceiling of the hall.

No seams. No trap door.

Frustrated, Nancy stood quiet a moment. She was sure she had heard something above her head. Maybe access to whatever lay above was through her room?

She went back, carefully closed the door, and looked around. There were no closets in the room—only a low chest of drawers, and a large old-fashioned wardrobe. As she ran the flashlight beam around the walls, she heard the noise again—coming from right above her bed.

Nancy checked the wall behind the dresser first, but found nothing. She turned her attention to the wardrobe. It was heavy, and for a moment she wondered if she should wait until morning and get some help moving it. But if someone was prowling around the attic, they'd be long gone by morning. It was obvious that however someone had gotten into the space above her, they hadn't gotten there through her room.

She put down her flashlight. Using all her strength, she was able to angle the wardrobe out slightly from the wall. It scraped the floorboards, and made a grating sound. The noise overhead stopped. Great, Nancy thought. Nothing like announcing to someone you're looking for them! But moving the wardrobe meant making noise. At least she'd have a chance to see what the prowler was up to. With another push, she angled the wardrobe out a full ninety degrees.

She reached for her flashlight and shone it on the wall. At first she didn't see anything. Just the same stained flowered wallpaper that covered the rest of the guest room. Then, as she felt around, her hand touched a latch. She'd found a secret door.

9

What Lies Above

Nancy studied the door a moment. Someone had clearly gone to great lengths to camouflage it. However, time and the settling of the house had done their work. The outline of a door showed clearly behind the wallpaper. When Jen and Jason got around to repapering this room, they would have found the entrance.

Nancy pressed her ear to the door but heard nothing. Whoever was skulking around upstairs had left by some other way out.

Using her penknife, Nancy cut through the wallpaper along the edges of the door. She tugged at the ring. It was stiff, and Nancy was afraid she might break it. She grabbed a credit card from her bag and worked it between the latch and the door. She tried again. The door groaned open, the hinges stiff and rusty.

Nancy had to bend to get through the low door. It opened immediately onto a steep staircase. It went up several steps past Nancy's room, and ended in a crawl space. It also continued down somewhere into the lower part of the house.

Maybe George had been right. Maybe Malone had been able to hide stuff away from the Feds before his arrest. A secret staircase, leading to a crawl space that subsequent house owners never even knew existed. Because, of course, it wouldn't have appeared on the plans.

Nancy headed up the steps to investigate the crawl space. The dust was thick, and huge cobwebs festooned the low rafters. The crawl space had a solid floor. Stacked haphazardly in a far corner was an assortment of intriguing suitcases and trunks.

Keeping her head low to avoid the beams, Nancy started toward the stack of luggage. Suddenly, a door slammed behind her!

She went back down the few steps and, sure enough, the door to her room had closed. The wind had probably just blown it shut. Heaving a frustrated sigh, Nancy felt for the latch.

There was none. This side of the door had no knob. She threw her weight against the door, but it wouldn't budge. "I don't believe this!" she exclaimed.

At least there was another way out of the crawl space. Aiming her flashlight on the steep, narrow stairs, Nancy started down. She'd find out where the staircase emerged.

As she neared the bottom, Nancy froze. A light was seeping under the door. Quickly she flicked off her flashlight. She tried to proceed quietly, but the stairs creaked with every step. She reached the last step and put her hand on the door.

Just as she touched it, there was the sudden sound of a bolt being thrown. The light went out, and Nancy found herself trapped.

"Let me out of here!" she shouted, banging on the door. But whoever was on the other side had locked her in on purpose. She stopped banging and pressed her ear to the door, but heard nothing. The prowler had probably already left the house.

Nancy went back up the stairs and began to pound on the door to her room. "George, Bess, Ned!" she yelled.

After a few minutes she heard footsteps racing into her room. She heard a light flick on and a sleepy voice calling her name: "Nancy?"

"Bess, look behind the wardrobe," Nancy shouted through the door.

"I don't believe this!" she heard George exclaim. "Where did this door come from?"

"At the moment it doesn't matter," Nancy told her.

"Just open it. There's no handle on this side. Be careful. It's stiff."

"I'm opening it now!" Ned said. "Stand back, Nan."

She stepped away from the door and listened to Ned straining to open it. Then after a second it creaked on its hinges. It flew open, the bright light in the room blinding Nancy as it flooded the dusty staircase.

"What happened?" Ned asked, as Nancy stepped into the bedroom. She was mad at whomever locked her in and was without a clue as to who it might have been.

She told them quickly about hearing the noises then finding the door. "The crazy part was the prowler was still here and locked me in from below."

George poked her head into the narrow stairwell. "Oh, I see it goes down from here. Let's go check."

"My thought exactly," Nancy said, "but first let's make sure we don't get locked up here."

Working together, they managed to wedge the wardrobe against the open stairway door so nothing could blow it shut again.

"Why don't I go downstairs? Then when you get to the door, start shouting, and I'll follow your voice, and we'll find out where the staircase leads," Ned suggested.

"Good thinking," Nancy said.

While Bess went with Ned, Nancy and George walked down the steps. "My guess," Nancy said, "is that this part of the house is near the pantry." When they reached the bottom they banged on the door. Within seconds they heard a bolt thrown, and the door opened—without a single squeak or creak.

"Someone oiled these hinges recently," Ned said, as Nancy and George stepped through the door and into the pantry.

"They probably thought this was the only entrance or exit. Unless you're actually looking for it, you'd miss the door that leads into my room. Even from the staircase side, it sits flush with the wall and has no handles," Nancy pointed out. "They wanted to be sure no one heard them coming or going. I'm sorry to disappoint you, Bess. Apparently the noises you were hearing—which *were* real—*weren't* made by a ghost."

"I figured that out by now." Bess shivered slightly in her light nightshirt. "But I can't say that knowing that someone has been creeping around right above our heads while we sleep makes me feel better."

"I hear you," George said, then looked around the pantry and frowned. "I don't think anyone's taken anything."

"Whoever it was made a run for it," Ned said. "I checked the porch just now. The screen door, which we always latch against the wind, was open."

"Maybe we should check out the yard," George suggested. "Remember, Bess thought she saw a prowler earlier, though when we checked, there was no one."

Right. Nancy had forgotten about that. Had it been the same person she'd followed into the woods before, triggering the Lawrence-Joneses' photo setup? Or was it someone else?

Nancy shook her head. "No point. They're long gone. But let's see what they were looking at upstairs. Ned, I'll need your help. We can carry the stuff I found down here to the kitchen. There's no electricity I could find up there, and there's lots to look through."

"I could use a chocolate fix," Bess said. "We're all awake already. We might as well stay up. I'll make hot chocolate."

Soon the four friends were seated in the breakfast nook, sorting through the old-fashioned suitcases. "I don't believe this stuff," Bess said. "I know George said Malone might have stowed loot here, but who'd have thought he would keep such pretty clothes?"

"They weren't *his* clothes, silly!" George teased. "Maybe they belonged to his girlfriend, or maybe he was married." She looked up at Nancy. "What do we know about this guy anyway?"

Nancy shrugged. "Not much. Just what Ravi told

us. He was a minor New York mob figure who built a hideaway here in the twenties or earlier, and then he was busted."

"Well, all I know is that these were found here in Jen and Jason's house, and they don't look like stolen property. I'm going to ask Jen if I can keep some of this stuff," Bess said. She jumped up and held a sheer pale green silk shirt up to her face and tried to catch her reflection in the breakfast nook window. "They may not be stolen jewels, but this stuff could fetch big bucks from a collector of period clothes. Everything's in such great condition," Bess concluded, carefully folding the shirt and putting it back in the suitcase.

"I'm sure Jen will let you have most of that stuff. Retro isn't her style, and you are the family's queen of antiques!" George teased. "Besides, that looked beautiful on you."

Nancy knelt beside the open trunk. "Something's weird about this," she said. "It's filled with mementos, but they're all the kinds of things a woman would keep: playbills, concert programs, dried flowers, even a couple of old-fashioned dolls. And"—she reached into the very bottom of the trunk—"a stash of old-fashioned lace tablecloths and other household linens."

George raised one eyebrow. "Looks like the kind of stuff my great-grandmother had. Everything seems like it's pretty high quality, and hardly used."

Nancy frowned. "Like Bess said, this stuff is probably worth something. But why would Mike Malone build a secret crawl space to house it? It makes no sense."

Bess reached for an old-fashioned hard-backed ladies' overnight bag. It was dark blue with a white striped pattern, and its leather handle had rotted through. "Oh, look at this!" she exclaimed with a delighted gasp. "All this old-fashioned makeup!"

Nancy got up and looked into the case Bess was unpacking. A trayful of cosmetics, little powder puffs, hair ornaments, and miscellaneous grooming items was nestled above a lower compartment. Carefully, Bess lifted the tray to reveal a bunch of letters. Nancy knew she'd finally stumbled on something of real interest.

"Love letters!" Bess touched the faded pink ribbon that half held them together. It had been untied, and Nancy carefully picked up the packet.

"Someone's been looking through these," Nancy declared.

"And you interrupted!" Ned observed.

"Probably, though I don't know how long this person was upstairs before the noise woke me up. Whoever it was didn't have much time to put this all away and disappear before I found the door."

"Maybe we'll find a clue as to who lived here," George said.

Carefully, Nancy began to look through the letters. The first thing she noticed was that the first few letters were arranged in date order, but the rest seemed to be stacked together randomly.

Nancy read the first few letters and looked up, her eyes bright with excitement. At last there was a clear connection. "These are all from Mike Malone to his fiancée, Nellie!"

"He was married?" Ned sounded surprised.

"Apparently . . . or he planned to be," Nancy said. "And the letters are only part love letters; part of every letter also recounts Malone's exploits with the mob to Nellie."

"That's pretty dangerous stuff to put in writing," Ned pointed out. "If the Feds ever found these letters, they would have had enough to put him away for life!"

"Which they did," George reminded him, "with or without the letters. I bet Emily would give her right arm to see these. This stuff is a real history of the day-to-day workings of bootleggers and hoodlums. Isn't that what Ravi said her long-term documentary was about?"

Nancy nodded. "Yes, Emily would love to see these. And we'll show them to her eventually. She had a pretty bad reaction to hearing Malone was connected with her new home."

"Who can blame her?" Ned laughed. "Talk about bringing work home with you. . . ."

Nancy was only half listening. Using the postmarks, she was carefully putting the letters in order by date. "There's a letter here every Tuesday and Thursday for well over two years, except for one gap toward the end of 1925, when two weeks' worth of letters are missing." Nancy looked from Bess to George to Ned. "Someone's been in here and taken one group of letters. But why?"

10

The Best Laid Plans

Nancy took a look through the remaining letters. "I'm just too tired to figure this out right now. Let's not tell anyone about these letters just yet—not even Emily. I want to do some research first. I'm headed off for a nap. When I wake up, I want to go into town and check out the Historical Society. In a small community like this—particularly back then—Malone must have been something of a local celebrity. I bet they still have records of his arrest on file."

Ned made a face. "I thought we might explore the lake with the boats today. George said two canoes came with the cabin and that Emily has one too. I was going to see if Ravi wanted to join us."

Nancy hated to see the disappointment in Ned's eyes. "You know I want to spend time with you. But I have to check this out, or it's going to drive me crazy." She turned to Bess and George. "Why don't you all go without me?"

"It won't be the same," George said. "And are you sure you don't want one of us along for the ride?"

"That's okay. I won't be in town long. Anyway, at the moment, I just need a nap!"

"We all do," Bess said with a yawn. "But we'd better lock up down here first, and maybe close that secret door to your room, Nancy. If the prowler comes back, we don't want him or her traipsing through that crawl space."

With that, Nancy went upstairs. But before she went to sleep, she carefully put the packet of letters in her knapsack.

Refreshed by a few hours' sleep, Nancy showered, and was in town before noon. The Lost Valley Historical Society was housed in the same sprawling Victorian mansion as the Native American museum where Jim worked. She was not in the mood for another run-in with him. It seemed every time they saw each other, something nasty happened, tempers flared, and Nancy ended up fighting mad. With any luck, he wouldn't be around.

Nancy climbed up the short flight of steps to the wraparound porch and discovered that the building had been renovated. There were two front doors: one leading to the Historical Society, the other to the Native American museum. The door to the museum was open, but a sign hung on the doorknob of the Historical Society saying that the Society was closed for lunch and would reopen at one. Nancy checked her watch. She had a twenty minute wait.

She wasn't sure what to do. Part of her was eager to visit the museum, but what if she ran into Jim? She hesitated for a minute. She wasn't going to let that guy's nasty attitude stop her from going.

Nancy walked through the open door into a spacious foyer lined with display cases. She continued on to a large open room. Along the walls were ancient and contemporary local native crafts—mainly Lenape. But Nancy's attention was quickly drawn to a diorama setup on a huge round table in the center of the room.

Posted at the front of the table was a simple sign. It read, BEFORE THE FLOOD. Nancy's curiosity soared when she realized it was a skillfully crafted reproduction of the valley in 1924.

Nancy quickly located the north shore. Sure enough, the diorama was so detailed, she easily located what must have been the whole Malone property. As Ravi said, it bordered a large beaver pond. The valley below was a regular patchwork of farms with fields, barns, and farmhouses. Small hamlets with church spires and tiny streets punctuated the sparsely populated landscape.

The Malone property bordered what was labeled as Lenape land. It was a small tract, but it ran right through the current dividing line between Emily's house and Camp Moonlight. And all of Camp Moonlight had originally belonged to the Lenape people. Malone's little compound showed the big house, the guest house, a toolshed—but no boathouse.

"That's the *before* picture! Now, how about the *after*!" a tight voice commented.

Nancy turned. "Jim!" she said, forcing back a wave of anger.

"We keep running into each other," he said, folding his arms across his chest. His whole being was a challenge to her—but Nancy decided not to be challenged. She was too curious about the valley and this diorama.

"This museum's pretty impressive," she said.

As she had hoped, her comment disarmed him slightly. "Now that I'm permanent staff, we have one full-time curator, then me and two assistants. We're getting things together, slowly but surely," he said, a note of real pride in his voice. "When my boss gets back from vacation, I'll be able to work full-time on 'Part Two' of this one."

"'Part Two' is after the flood?" Nancy asked, immediately wanting to bite back her words as she realized Jim thought she was mocking him.

"Yeah, what else," Jim said, tensing up again. "If you're interested, it's in the next room. It's still pretty much a work in progress."

Nancy was surprised at his offer, and quickly took him up on it. He led her into a room that abutted the Historical Society's half of the building. A broad, open arched doorway separated the two institutions.

"Now, this should look more familiar," he said, drawing back a protective cloth from the top of a large display table.

The whole north shore of the lake looked pretty complete to Nancy, though the east, west, and south shores were still blocked out with brown terraform material and lots of Post-it notes. Nancy quickly spotted the Fayne cottage, Emily's house, Camp Moonlight, and then on the other side of the Faynes', a nearly completed model of the Lawrence-Joneses' cabin. Map locator pins dotted parts of the forest, the grounds of Camp Moonlight, the Fayne cottage, and Emily's yard. Some of the pins went right down into the replicated lake.

"What are these?" she asked Jim.

"None of your business," he snapped.

Nancy rolled her eyes. This guy kept acting as if *she* were personally responsible for flooding the valley and disturbing his ancestral lands. "What's with you?" she started to ask but just then a woman poked her head through the door to the Historical Society's side of the building.

"I'm back, Jim. I'm officially open now. You don't need to watch the shop," the woman said.

Jim gave her a thumbs-up and walked away from Nancy.

The whole reason Nancy had come to town was to check out the Historical Society. "Excuse me, but I actually came here to check out some of your records," Nancy said to the woman.

"Of course. Come in. Sorry I was still at lunch—but I hope Jim kept you entertained," the woman said, flicking on the lights in the front room. Before tucking her purse inside her desk, she pulled out her compact and checked her hair. She was an attractive woman with a friendly smile.

Nancy decided not to respond to her remark about Jim. "My name's Nancy Drew, and I'm staying with friends at the cottage on the old Malone property on the north shore."

"Mike Malone's old place? Yes, I know the cottage. It's charming! I hear a young couple bought it about a year or so ago. And then the Malone house itself just got sold after being on the market for a good five years. Amazing—when things start happening, they happen fast," she babbled on. "Oh, by the way, my name's Karen Kopekski. I more or less run this place, together with a really great committee of volunteers."

Nancy smiled. She'd have to talk fast to get a word in edgewise; Karen was such a talker. "Anyway," Nancy said, unzipping her knapsack, "I found these letters in the cottage last night. Apparently there's a secret stairway in the house that leads to a—"

"You don't say!" Karen looked thrilled.

"To a crawl space," Nancy continued. "I went through the letters a bit last night. They were all written by Mike Malone, but I wondered if your records here could shed some light on them."

"Oh my, those would be of great interest to the Society," Karen said. "Mike Malone is a real local celebrity. In fact, there have been rumors circulating for years that he's still haunting the old main house. Of course, that's only if you believe in ghosts. But if you do"—Karen giggled—"there are supposedly at least ten of them wandering around the north shore. Why the ghosts of farmers who lived twenty-five miles away down in the valley would bother to haunt the north shore is beyond me. Back in the mid-twenties, it was mainly Native American land. Traveling twenty-five miles in these parts was quite an excursion."

"Would you tell me how the local Native American groups feel about Moonlight Lake now?" Nancy asked.

Karen shrugged. "Mostly just like everyone else.

They use it for recreation: boating, fishing, water sports. There are a few who still resent the way the tribal lands were more or less ripped out from under them by the powers behind the hydroelectric projects."

"People like Jim?"

"Yes, but at least he's channeled his anger in good directions. He's going through the courts trying to get property owners on this side of the lake to set aside a small area—a memorial really—to the native people who lived in the region for hundreds of years before the white man came."

Nancy wanted to learn more about Jim's project, but she could see that Karen was eagerly eyeing the packet of letters.

"Can we look at those now?" Karen asked, pulling a second chair up to the desk and putting on a pair of reading glasses.

Nancy sat down, and for a good twenty minutes they pored over the letters.

"Now, this is interesting," Karen said, in a serious voice. "Back here in 1923, Malone's written something about plans for a boathouse, and a chance for serious boating coming up. . . ."

"What's wrong with that?" Nancy asked.

Karen peered at Nancy over her glasses. "Well, he doesn't spell it out, Nancy, but I think Malone had foreknowledge of the flooding of the valley. The plans were top-secret until late in 1924. The minute they were made public, a huge controversy erupted. But since this was a poor, underpopulated area, the power company and state won easily."

Nancy leaned back and thought a moment. "Malone was a mobster, notoriously in cahoots with corrupt politicians. He probably had inside knowledge of lots of things."

"But what's even more interesting is that he mentions plans. Our town archives have plans dating from the last years of the nineteenth century. Come on, let's look and see what we can find."

Nancy jumped at the chance. Karen took Nancy into the Historical Society's library. Plans were stored in large wooden flat-files, sorted first by date, then title of property. They searched several years before 1923 and after 1925 but they couldn't find the plans.

Karen was visibly disappointed. "I *so* hoped to find them. You know, Jim's 1924 diorama has no boathouse—but now we have no idea when it was built. A builder would have had to file plans."

"Malone might not have wanted to tip his hand that he knew about the flooding of the valley ahead of time," Nancy reasoned. "And maybe he didn't have to file plans. He certainly had the connections to build a boathouse without the locals objecting."

"Do you think the plans are still in the house?" Karen asked.

"I don't know. They weren't with the letters. . . ." Nancy thought for a moment. Had they been under that pried-up plank in the pantry? The space was narrow but long, and a tube of rolled up architectural drawings could have easily fit there.

Karen suddenly looked up past Nancy's shoulder. "Jim, how long have you been standing there?" she asked pleasantly.

"Didn't want to interrupt you guys," he said. He had a definite smirk on his face. How much had he heard?

"I'm heading to lunch now," he said, his voice neutral. "So if you would keep an eye on things . . ."

"Of course, Jim. You just go on ahead." Karen waved him away.

As he left the room, Nancy noticed he was wearing the same sheathed knife in his belt and was carrying the same sort of burlap sack over his shoulder that she'd seen in the back of his truck the day before.

Nancy drove home, her mind reeling from the wealth of new information. Her first thought was of Jim. How long had he been eavesdropping? She tried to tell herself she was being paranoid about him; after all, except for his attitude and bad driving habits, he hadn't done anything *truly* suspicious.

100

Or had he? His reaction to her question about those locator tacks on the post-flood diorama had been pretty extreme. He didn't want her to know whatever they stood for. And that smirk on his face when Karen discovered him listening at the library door—Nancy's gut instinct told her the guy knew something about that boathouse, if not the letters.

When Nancy got back to the cottage, Bess, George, and Ned were still out boating with Ravi. After downing a glass of milk and a couple of cookies, Nancy decided to go find Emily and tell her what she found out about the history of the boathouse and the Malone property.

As she headed outside, she saw the hauling and excavation truck parked in the driveway. She walked around the various sheds and outbuildings, but didn't see Emily anywhere. She was probably off with Dale and Kevin, supervising some project.

Passing the boathouse, Nancy noticed that the door was open. She looked inside. "Emily, you there?" she called. But a quick look around revealed that the place was empty. Two cups of coffee sat on a workbench. Nancy went over and touched the cups; they were still warm. Strange, she thought.

Nancy decided to come back later, but as she started to leave, she caught sight of a plank straddling two sawhorses. Tacked to the plank were some sort of architectural drawings. Probably renovation plans. Curious, she went to take a closer look.

Up close, she could see that the paper was old, and the plans seemed hand-drawn—much like several of the plans she'd looked at with Karen back at the Historical Society library.

Leaning closer, she saw the architect's signature, and the date in the lower right-hand corner read: SEPTEMBER, 1923.

Nancy couldn't believe her eyes! Was this the plan for the boathouse that Mike Malone had never filed? Suspicion surged in Nancy's mind, but she took a breath. Emily had every right to these plans. She probably found them in her own house, and was using them to guide her renovations.

As Nancy studied the plans, something struck her as odd. Little arrows were drawn from the beach of the cottage, from the dock of the main house, and from the lawn, down into the water. Other arrows pointed to a corner of the boathouse itself, the part that seemed to have been badly damaged over the years. Nancy had noticed yesterday how the stones along one corner had been pulled out, and how that corner of the boathouse was propped up with some type of beam.

Nancy looked more closely at all the arrows: they were drawn in ballpoint pen—a kind of pen that didn't exist in 1923. Closer inspection revealed they were carefully traced over faded pencil marks.

What did those arrows mean?

The thought had barely formed in her mind when suddenly a strong, calloused hand gripped her wrist hard and shoved her to the ground. As her head struck the corner of the table, Nancy blacked out.

11

A Familiar Prowler

She slowly surfaced back to consciousness and felt the touch of cool hands on her face.

"Nancy!" A vaguely familiar voice was calling her name.

Nancy opened her eyes and found herself looking up into Emily's face. The woman looked pale and scared half to death. "I'm okay, Emily. Really." Nancy started to sit up. The movement made her stomach lurch, but she fought back the wave of nausea. Holding Emily's arm, she slowly managed to get to her feet. She wasn't quite sure where she was—some sort of shed.

"What in the world happened?" Emily asked, guiding Nancy over to an upturned barrel. Nancy sat down and massaged her temple. She had fallen somehow and hit her head.

Careful to move slowly, Nancy looked around. Gradually, the room came into focus. Broken glass littered a windowsill. Coils of old rope, oars, and life jackets hung on the walls. I'm in the boathouse, she realized. Suddenly everything rushed back to her. She'd been looking at old boathouse plans when someone had grabbed her from behind. She could still feel the calloused hands on her wrist. Whoever it was knocked her down—or knocked her out.

She stood up slowly. For a moment the walls of the boathouse seemed to spin.

"You don't look so good," Emily warned.

"I'm okay. I just remembered what happened," Nancy said in a sober tone. "Emily, I was looking at the boathouse plans, when someone came up behind me and knocked me out."

"Boathouse plans?" Emily asked.

Nancy pointed to the sawhorses and the old plank door that served as a work surface. The plans were gone. "He must have made off with them."

Emily's eyes widened. "I don't believe this," she gasped in horror. "Why in the world would someone steal those?" She exhaled forcefully and marched over to the boathouse door. When she turned to face Nancy she looked like she was about to cry. "That means I have to have them redrawn. My budget's so tight, but I've already contracted the work—"

"Why *would* someone want those plans?" Nancy asked.

"Beats me," Emily said. "Except maybe to cause me trouble. Everyone and his uncle around here knows I spent too much for this place and is waiting for me to default on the mortgage."

"But that doesn't mean people want to cause you that much grief," Nancy said.

"You wouldn't think so, would you?" Emily plunked herself down on the barrel and buried her face in her hands for a moment. "But there seems to be an army of people who resent my being here. I just try to ignore them and pretend they don't exist," she said slowly. "First of all, there's that guy from the Native American museum, Jim. He's been causing grief for everyone on the north shore. He seems to think present landowners owe his ancestors something for having bought the land. He hassles everyone and is always creeping around the woods—even if he's trespassing on other people's land. I keep finding these weird piles of stones all over the place. The other day there was one on my lawn. Dale told me they give him the creeps and mumbled something about spirit totems. The guy's weird, and he's mad at everyone who lives here."

"I think I know what you're talking about," Nancy

said. Had Jim been building some kind of spirit cairn when she and Ned ran into him in the woods?

"Then there's Steve Delmonico," Emily said. "He's furious I bought this place out from under him, even though he was taking forever to decide to buy. He'd love to see me fail here, believe me. He's ready to jump in and buy the place from the bank."

"I heard about that," Nancy told her. "And have you had any trouble with George and Bess's neighbors? The Lawrence-Joneses are upset about all the commotion on the lake this summer. They keep talking about boats paddling around at night disturbing the geese. And some kind of drilling noise."

Emily snapped to attention. "Drilling?" Her voice sounded strained.

"Yeah—I haven't heard it myself, but the past two nights . . ." Nancy shook her head. "So much has gone on, I might not have noticed."

"I'm not sure what they're talking about. Maybe something over at the camp. I guess I sleep too soundly to hear," Emily said. Then she looked at Nancy. "You're looking better. Hey—how come you were here, in the boathouse, anyway?"

Nancy laughed. "I came looking for you. I spent the morning at the Lost Valley Historical Society and wanted to tell you what I found out about the boathouse and the old Malone property. I thought you might be able to fill in some of the blanks." She reached for her backpack. "And because of these!" She produced the bundle of letters. The burglar hadn't been interested in Nancy's backpack or wallet—just in the plans. Nancy decided she'd think about that later. She handed the letters to Emily.

"Look what I found in the cottage. Turns out there's this secret crawl space that was never in the cottage plans. It has two hidden entrances."

Emily stared at the bundle. When she looked back up at Nancy, her face was flushed. "I-I don't understand. What do these have to do with me?"

Nancy frowned. Emily's reaction wasn't quite what she'd expected.

"They're from Mike Malone to his fiancée, Nellie. I thought you'd be interested in them for your work."

Emily gave an embarrassed laugh. "Oh—of course." She paused and asked, "You've read them?"

"You bet I have. They're partly love letters, but what should interest you more is how they detail the inside workings of the mob at that time. I bet if you ask Jennifer and Jason, they'll let you copy them to use in your film."

"That's a great idea," Emily said.

"Anyway, I think whoever stole the boathouse plans was after these too," Nancy explained.

"What makes you say that?"

"Well, although everything else in the old trunks and suitcases we found was in very good order—

the blouses were still packed away with old tis_e
paper between them—these letters had been d_i
turbed. The bow was untied, and a group of letters
was missing."

"How could you possibly tell that letters were
missing?" Emily asked.

Nancy explained about how she arranged them
and discovered a two-week break in correspondence.

"But maybe they've been missing a long time,
Nancy. You said these were love letters. Maybe a few
got too personal. Maybe Nellie destroyed them."

"I hadn't thought of that," Nancy admitted. Emily
had a point, but that didn't explain why someone was
rooting around the crawl space in the middle of the
night. Or why he or she made sure to trap Nancy inside. Then she remembered what else she wanted to
ask Emily. "Last night, you said you didn't know
much about Mike Malone, but I was wondering—
did he ever marry this Nellie person?"

"Absolutely!"

Her answer was so sure and definite, Nancy was
taken aback. "I thought you didn't know much about
him."

Emily bit her lip and laughed. "I didn't. Ravi really
embarrassed me last night. So I hit the Internet today
and did some research. I guess that fact stood out.
Goons like Malone usually had a string of hanger-on
girlfriends; their molls. But Malone seemed to have

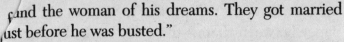

and the woman of his dreams. They got married just before he was busted."

Nancy was glad to hear that. His letters to Nellie were surprisingly tender. Reading them, it had been hard to remember he was a cold-blooded killer.

"Excuse me, ladies." One of the workmen poked his head in the door. He stared at Nancy a moment, then at Emily. "I'm leaving for the day."

"Were you able to find some suitable stones to patch up that corner of the boathouse?" Emily asked.

"Yep, that we did. Like you said, there were plenty that were just the right size in the old stone wall at the back of your property. We'll haul them out early tomorrow morning, if that's okay with you."

"Sounds great," Emily said. "See you later, Kevin."

"Sure thing," he said, turning to go. At the door he turned. "By the way, was that Indian guy hassling you again? He was skulking around the boathouse earlier."

"You mean Jim?" Nancy asked, curious.

Kevin gave Emily a knowing look. "Emily knows who I mean; the guy who's asking for trouble and who's going to get it."

12

Shadows in the Moonlight

Jim? Instantly, Nancy tried to remember Jim's hands. Were they calloused? She hadn't noticed them before.

"I didn't see him," Emily said, "but maybe Nancy did. Maybe it was someone else who's the same height as Jim."

Kevin shook his head. "Nope. It was that crazy activist. Believe me, I'd recognize him from ten miles away . . . aw, well, maybe not quite." Tugging at the bill of his cap, Kevin went to the door. "Just thought you should know, Emily."

Kevin had barely walked out the door when Emily slapped her forehead. "Sorry, but all this commotion got me scrambled—I have to pay the guys!" She started to leave, then turned to Nancy. "You okay now? If you wait, I'll walk you home."

111

"I'm fine. Nothing an aspirin won't cure. But maybe you should warn Kevin about the missing plans. Doesn't he need them for his work?"

"I didn't think of that," Emily gasped. "I'd better go tell him about the plans now, before he and Dale split."

Nancy left the boathouse with Emily, then headed back toward the cottage. Why would Jim want to burgle the boathouse? Then she remembered him hanging around outside the Historical Society library, listening to her talk about the missing plans.

She kicked slowly through the grass, and tried to recall those ballpoint pen markings on the old drawings. Were they related to Jim's locator markers back on the post-flood diorama? Nancy couldn't remember enough about the pen marks to even hazard a guess.

Maybe the old plans would bolster his argument about the moral obligation of contemporary north shore landowners to help preserve some of the native lands—though frankly, Nancy couldn't imagine how.

"*NANCEEEEEEE!*" The shout rang out from the direction of the lake.

Nancy turned. She spotted George and Ned in the Faynes' canoe, and saw Bess with Ravi in one of Emily's rowboats. They were paddling toward shore at a furious pace.

Had something bad happened?

As they drew closer to shore, Nancy could see everyone was smiling. George and Ned reached the Faynes' dock first, while Ravi rowed toward Emily's short pier. As Ned tied up the canoe, George jogged up to Nancy. She wore a loose striped shirt over her swimsuit. "You won't believe it. We found the absolute best place in the world for a sunset picnic!"

"Out on that island, Nan," Ned said. "There's even a barbecue setup. Apparently, it's part of the state park. There are hiking trails and the best view of the lake. Bess and George decided it would be the perfect dinner spot."

Nancy lit up. "That sounds like fun."

"Why don't you change into your bathing suit?" Ned suggested as Bess trudged toward them from the direction of Emily's lawn. She waved good-bye to Ravi and shouted over her shoulder, "See you later, right?"

Ravi gave her a thumbs-up sign. "Wouldn't miss it."

"Bess is once again smitten—except she hasn't been able to figure out the story between Ravi and Emily," George whispered. Nancy had to smile.

"So what do we do about food?" Nancy asked as they trooped together up the back steps.

"We've got tons of stuff—hot dogs, buns, chips, you name it. We'll pack it up while you change," George promised. Within the hour, they were back in their boats and headed for the island.

The only disappointment was Ravi. Emily came alone, rowing over with Bess, and bringing her own modest stash of picnic treats.

"So why couldn't Ravi make it?" Nancy asked as she threw some hot dogs on the grill.

"It's the wildest thing," Emily said. "I happened to tell Dale about Ravi's project, since Dale's kind of into the drowned-valley-ghost thing himself," she added with a tolerant laugh. "Anyway, turns out Dale knows about this elderly woman—she might even be close to a hundred years old—who lives in a town about fifty miles from here. She knows a ton about the history of this place. Ravi found her number, and she said she'd be happy to talk to him, *if* he could visit before nine tomorrow morning. So he's going to drive down there, stay at a motel, and visit her. He felt he couldn't pass that up."

While George and the others manned the grill, Nancy took the opportunity to take a walk with Ned. They chose a trail that wound up toward the high point of the small island. It was a low windswept hill. On top there were remains of many bonfires. Nancy and Ned sat down to enjoy the view. They propped their backs against a large rock and watched the sun swing low over the western horizon.

"So what happened today in town?" Ned asked. "We haven't had a chance to catch up."

Nancy put her thoughts together and told Ned

about the two dioramas, the map locator tacks, and her visit with Karen and their search of the Historical Society library.

"What was Emily's reaction when you told her about the plans and the letters?" Ned asked.

"Well, that all got pretty complicated," Nancy said, and she related the story about being attacked in the boathouse.

"This is getting serious," Ned said firmly. "Maybe we should call in the cops."

"To report that a plan was stolen?" Nancy shook her head.

"Yes," Ned insisted. "Especially since whatever this burglar is up to is escalating. Last night he locked you in the attic. Today, he attacked you."

"But is it the same person, Ned? I can't figure out the connection between the letters and the plans—but I am positive there is one, no matter what Emily says."

"Maybe the cottage burglar was looking for something else," Ned suggested.

"That's what I keep thinking. Maybe the plans? But they were right there in Emily's house all along. And for the past few weeks at least, they've been in her boathouse to help her work crew." Then suddenly, the pieces of the puzzle seemed to fall into place for Nancy. She grabbed Ned's arm. "Because until today no one knew they were there!"

"So who just found out?"

Nancy took a deep breath. "Jim. He overheard me talking with Karen about the boathouse and the missing plans."

Ned whistled under his breath, then regarded Nancy carefully. "But why, Nan? What's in it for him? I mean, plans for a boathouse?"

"That's what's bothering me—motive. Jim's got to have a pretty strong one to start breaking the law, particularly when he's been spearheading a Native American rights campaign around here." Nancy paused. "But one of Emily's workmen saw Jim hanging around the boathouse this afternoon."

Ned looked sharply at Nancy. "What a creep that guy is."

"I guess so." Something inside Nancy wasn't convinced, but the facts certainly did point to Jim.

Just then George called them to join the picnic.

"Ned, please don't tell everyone else about this just yet. Not until I'm sure," Nancy said as they descended the hill, hand in hand.

"Okay," Ned promised reluctantly. "But it's going to be hard not to give Jim a taste of his own medicine if I catch him lurking around again."

After doing justice to the hot dogs, chips, and Emily's salad, the friends built a bonfire on the beach and began making s'mores under the light of a full moon. Just outside the ring of fire, the air had a crisp early autumn feel to it. Nancy pulled on a gray hooded sweatshirt.

"So I guess Nancy didn't tell you about what we saw up on the hill, Bess," Ned said, gingerly plucking a sticky marshmallow off his stick.

"No. I thought maybe you were watching the sunset."

"That too, Bess," Nancy said, her eyes sparkling. She had a feeling she knew what Ned was up to.

"But just after sunset, we saw these strange lights, flickering far, far out across the lake, and then there was this cry—it was thin and distant, like a wail—and all at once, the lights went out!" Ned intoned in a spooky voice.

Bess shuddered and wrapped her arms around herself. She was snuggled in her oversized pink cotton sweater. She looked out over the lake toward shore and suddenly screamed. "Look! Your lights. They're back again!"

Ned started to laugh, but Nancy jumped up and pulled out her binoculars. Sure enough, Bess was right. There really was one light, and a low, droning sound coming from the shadowy form of a flat-bottomed boat pulling right into Emily's dock. Nancy's binoculars weren't geared for the dark, but her vision was keen. Moonlight flickered around the dark shadow on the lake, and she thought she saw the outline of two figures. The engine cut off, and the boat drifted into deep shadow. For a moment, Nancy wasn't sure her eyes hadn't been playing tricks on her. But a moment later, the boat moved stealthily away from the dock in the direction of the inlet on the other side of Camp Moonlight.

"Emily," Nancy gasped and pulled the woman to her feet. Emily resisted slightly, but in seconds, Nancy was bringing her down to the shoreline. "Come here. Someone's broken into your boathouse again! Look, that boat just pulled up to your pier. Someone went into your boathouse, and is leaving now." Even as she spoke, the boat drifted into the shadows near the shore. Then suddenly the engine started up again, and the boat disappeared around the strip of land, out of view of the island.

Nancy turned toward Emily. Instead of looking at the island, she was staring at Nancy. In the dim light of the bonfire behind them, Nancy couldn't quite read her expression.

"Emily, didn't you see that? Someone broke into your boathouse again. Whoever attacked me this afternoon came back!"

"I-I didn't see, but I believe you." Emily's reaction was delayed. She leaned in to Nancy. "What's happening here? Why is everyone against my being here?"

"What's going on?" George said, offering them each some s'mores.

"Nancy saw a boat out there. At first I thought it

118

was just a figment of Bess's imagination, thanks to Ned," Emily said. "But then I *did* see something, or at least *hear* something."

"It was probably those crazy bird watching folks. Bet they saw some rare night-fishing bird, and tracked it to your boathouse. You better hope it doesn't *nest* there, or they'll try to stop your renovations," George warned with a smile.

Nancy frowned. "That's possible." She hadn't mentioned the robbery of the plans yet to her friends, and she hoped Emily wouldn't now.

"Maybe we'd better tramp down the fire and go back now," Nancy suggested, turning toward Emily.

"Uh—sure. That's a good idea. Though I bet George is right. A lot of birds nest over in that inlet, and the boat was headed in that direction."

After packing up and making sure that their barbecue fire had died down and the bonfire was completely out, they headed straight for shore. Nancy suggested they all go to the cottage first and unpack the food; then, she'd help Emily carry the light metal rowboat back to the main house.

Twenty minutes later, Nancy and Emily propped the rowboat against the side of the boathouse. "We can leave it here for the night," Emily suggested.

"I don't think so," Nancy said, wondering where Emily's head was. "You've been burgled at least once today. Someone could just make off with the boat."

119

"I doubt anyone's after my boat," Emily said with a shrug. "But you've got a point." She went to the shed and pulled out a large electric lantern. "Hold this," she told Nancy as she easily opened the boathouse door and propped the boat inside. Nancy peered over Emily's shoulder through the open door. "Is anything missing?"

"Not that I can tell. Of course, if someone ripped off one of the small tools, I wouldn't notice until the next time I needed it."

Emily simply closed the boathouse door behind her. "Aren't you going to lock it?" Nancy asked.

"The lock's been missing since yesterday. I misplaced it, and I haven't had a chance to get another," Emily explained. "Now, Nancy, don't look at me that way. I'm under a lot of pressure around here these days, and I can't remember everything. I'll get one tomorrow, I promise."

"Should I walk you back to the house?" Nancy offered.

Emily looked at her as if she'd grown two heads. "No way. If it's safe enough for you to walk home alone, it's safe enough for me. If someone *was* prowling around here, they're long gone."

"Okay. Take care!" Nancy said, then headed back past the dock. The moonlight was bright enough to making the going easy. She was almost past the dock when she noticed a pair of wet footprints leading up the sand and onto the dock. They were large and heavy, and were definitely made by a man wearing muddy work boots.

"So I was right!" she whispered to herself. Nancy bent down to examine the prints. One set traveled up from the shoreline, onto the dock, then into the grass. But it was obvious that whoever had come to shore had gone into the boathouse. She was about to continue around to the side of the boathouse to see if the prints indeed ended at the door, when she heard the low hum of a motor and the sound of muffled voices.

Nancy ducked behind a bush. She spotted two people in the boat. From her angle she couldn't tell if they were both male or not. Was it Caspar and Millicent, or someone else? The people kept talking and pointed over toward Emily's house. Nancy's heart stopped. Emily was in danger.

Before she could process that thought, she heard a rustling in the brush behind her. She spun around. It was Jim. His hair was wet, and he had a hunting knife in one hand—aimed directly at her.

13

Drowning in Moonlight

Nancy's reaction was immediate. She aimed a high karate kick at Jim's arm. The knife flew out of his hand, but he neatly sidestepped the blow.

He's trained in martial arts! Nancy realized, quickly moving out of his reach—but she was not fast enough. Jim reached out. As his hand gripped her wrist, she felt his calloused fingers.

"Hey!" he shouted. His cry rang out. Someone cursed loudly in the boat just offshore.

The curse distracted Jim, and Nancy wrenched free of his grasp. She spotted the knife gleaming in the damp grass and kicked it into the bushes, out of reach.

Jim glared at her. "What did you do that for?"

"You're kidding, right?" Nancy stared at him in

disbelief. "You just tried to attack me."

"I wasn't attacking you! I was keeping you from getting into some big trouble here. Weird stuff's been happening around here at night, in case you haven't noticed." The words were no sooner out of Jim's mouth than an outboard motor roared into life. The mystery boat took off across the lake.

Instinctively, Nancy turned at the sound. Through a break in the trees, she saw a small, flat-bottomed boat head out into the middle of the lake and vanish in the shadows. When she turned again, Jim was gone. He had disappeared into the brush.

A shiver ran down Nancy's spine. The guy moved as quietly as a cat. She decided to go right to Emily's to warn her about Jim. But before she headed up to the main house, she pulled out her penlight and searched the bushes for Jim's knife. It was gone. He had somehow managed to retrieve it when her back was turned. Great, she thought, he's armed!

Hands jammed into the pocket of her sweatshirt, Nancy hurried up the sloping lawn toward Emily's house. A neat rectangle of light from the kitchen window splashed the lawn. The rest of the house was dark.

Nancy went around to the back entrance, walked right into the mudroom, and almost tripped on something. She looked down and saw some sort of diving gear. A pair of wet flippers stuck out from underneath a bench. On top of the bench was a milk crate filled with old junk covered in green slime: an egg beater, a rusty hammer, a saw, and some broken pottery. It was the kind of stuff that someone would find in Timothy's Trash and Treasures. The stuff had obviously been dredged up from the lake—tonight, from the looks of it.

What was this stuff doing in Emily's mudroom? Nancy realized just then that voices were coming from the kitchen. Was Ravi back?

After a moment's hesitation, she walked into the room.

Emily wasn't with Ravi; she was with Dale. He wore a sweatshirt and jeans, and had work boots on. His hair was wet. A towel hung over the back of the chair.

"What are you doing here?" Emily gasped, her hand flying to her chest in surprise. "I thought you went home."

"I started to," Nancy said, then she explained about her encounter with Jim.

"Man—he came at you with a knife? That guy's gone too far!" Dale grumbled. "Want me to go after him?" he asked Emily.

"I wouldn't bother," Nancy told the workman. "He's probably long gone. The guy can move through the woods like a cat."

Dale nodded. "Tell me about it. We're always running into him, rooting around for something. I keep chasing him off Emily's land, but he waits until we've left, and then he comes back."

"Anyway, I wanted to warn you about him. I didn't like the idea of you being here alone tonight," Nancy said.

Emily looked sheepish. "Actually, that's why I called Dale. After seeing that boat hanging around my dock, I decided that maybe I shouldn't be out here all by myself."

Dale nodded. "I told Emily weeks ago that if she ever had trouble here, I'd come over and kind of guard the place. I'm going to check the grounds now."

Nancy regarded Dale skeptically. Between his wet hair and the stash of dredged-up junk lying in plain view in the mudroom, she wasn't sure he was telling the truth—or at least, not the whole truth.

Still, whatever they were up to was their business. From what George had told her, Nancy knew Emily was close to broke and probably had trouble making ends meet. Maybe they *were* dredging up junk illegally and selling it to junk and antique dealers.

At least Emily wouldn't be alone in the house.

"I think that's a great idea, Dale," Nancy said. "I don't know what Jim is up to. Maybe he was the prowler we saw before, or maybe whoever stole those plans is back looking for something else. But it's best for someone to be here, at least until Ravi gets back."

"Right," Emily said. "Ravi. He's due back late tomorrow."

"This was a great idea, George," Nancy said the next morning. While Bess and Ned slept in late, the two girls had set off on a hike through the woods. George suggested exploring the forest between the cottage and the Lawrence-Joneses' property. It was early, and the woods were filled with birdsong. The air was cool and fresh. Soon after they set out, Nancy filled George in on the events of the night before.

"Nan, you're right-on about Jim," George said when Nancy finished her story. "Let me show you something. When I was hiking around here last week before you guys came, I began finding some really weird things."

"Like what?" Nancy asked, as she scrambled up a low, rocky hill after George.

"Like this," George said, pointing to a cairn of smooth gray rocks. They lay at the base of a delicate paper birch tree. The rocks had been carefully chosen, and Nancy noted they were almost symmetrical and arranged in a kind of low pyramid. She crouched down and looked closely at the cairn. She touched the rocks and shrugged.

126

"Jim was building something like this over on Emily's property," Nancy said. "It doesn't seem very threatening."

George giggled. "No, of course not. And at first I thought it was sort of cool. I didn't tell Bess, of course, particularly when all the spooky stuff began happening. But *this* is really weird," George said, leading Nancy deeper into the forest. "Look in there," George said, pointing into a shallow cave at the base of a cliff.

Nancy stooped down. The cave was shadowed by trees, so Nancy pulled her penlight out of her pocket. She turned it on and grimaced at the sight before her. A small animal skull was in the center of the little cave. Some charred wood and a bundle of tiny bones tied together with a cord were carefully arranged a few inches from the skull. "It's some kind of fetish or spirit object," Nancy guessed.

George nodded. "Probably, but Jim's trespassing and being so mysterious about it all is making me wonder if he's doing this on purpose to spook people out."

"But why?" Nancy couldn't quite make sense of Jim's motives. While his hostility to everyone on this end of the lake was more than obvious, it wasn't enough to prove that he was responsible for the weird things that were happening. He was fighting a battle in court to try to redesignate part of the north shore as sacred land, because of ancestral burial sites. His fetishes and cairns were on other people's property—but that didn't make them particularly threatening. "Something about Jim just doesn't add up," she told George, thinking about the night before. Jim had practically assaulted her, but then he told her he was trying to protect her. From what? From the people in the boat?

And what about the people in the boat? Last night as she went to sleep, she had thought maybe it was Dale, but he couldn't have gotten back to Emily's house so quickly from the boat. Jim seemed to think that whoever was paddling around in the dark was dangerous. Had he just been trying to put her off? Was he teamed up with the prowler who Nancy and Emily had spied from the island earlier?

Nancy sighed as they backed out of the shallow cave and continued walking through the woods. Heading back down the hill, they meandered along a deer trail that descended toward the lake.

"Now *this* tree has to be really old!" George commented, patting the huge trunk of a towering oak. "Nothing's this big around here, except on a couple of the lawns!"

Nancy stopped to admire the stately tree. It towered high into the forest canopy. Its trunk was thick, and Nancy trailed her hand against the bark as she walked around it. Suddenly her fingers encountered the edge of a wooden slat. "Would you look at this!" she said. The slat was one of several hammered into the side of the massive tree. These formed a kind of ladder leading up to a gray weathered platform which was half concealed with newly cut branches from the tree.

"Some kind of observation point?" George suggested. "The Lawrence-Joneses' property is near here."

"Makes sense," Nancy said, carefully starting up the ladder. Moments later, Nancy reached the platform and gasped. Lying in full view was Jim's hunting knife, half out of its leather sheath.

14

A Ghostly Fleet

Nancy stuffed the knife in her knapsack, and she and George headed back to the house. Nancy hadn't made up her mind what to do about the knife, but she was tempted to call the police.

Just as they reached the house, Ravi's red Volkswagen roared into their driveway. He jumped out, leaving the engine running, and hurried over to Nancy.

"Where's Emily?" he asked, breathless.

"At the house, right?" Nancy said.

Ravi shook his head. Just then, Ned came out onto the lawn. His hair was wet, and his cheeks were pink from the shower. "Hi, guys, what's up?"

"Have you seen Emily?" Nancy asked Ned.

"Sure. She and Bess went into town. Emily suddenly had some urgent errand, and Bess wanted to check out something at the junk shop."

Ravi groaned. "I found out the most *incredible* thing and—wait until Emily hears!" He went over to the car and turned off the engine.

"Is it private?" Nancy asked, curious as to why Ravi was so charged.

"I'll tell you all about it if you give me coffee," Ravi said with a weary grin. "I'm working with a severe sleep deficit here."

"We'll even give you breakfast," George promised.

A few minutes later, they were all on the deck. Nancy and George sipped juice while Ned and Ravi dug into a plateful of bagels. Ravi sipped some of his coffee, then started his tale.

"You know how Dale told me there was this woman around here who was close to a hundred years old and remembered the place before it was flooded?"

"Sure, that's why you took off last night," Nancy commented, propping her feet on the railing.

"Turns out she lived much farther away than Dale said. She was in a town about seventy miles from here, quite far from the lake. Anyway, I ended up visiting her this morning. Her name's Betty Sue MacGregor. Turns out she had more information than I know what to do with."

"About the flooding of the valley?" Ned asked.

Ravi nodded. "Her recollections are interesting. She has scrapbooks about the whole process. I was looking through them when I came across some really wild information. It's about Mike Malone."

Nancy lowered her feet and leaned forward in her chair. "*Our* Mike Malone—the same gangster who owned Emily's house and this cottage?"

"The very person," Ravi said. "The clippings in the scrapbook didn't spell any of this out—only that the FBI suspected Malone had something stashed away at the house. But Ms. MacGregor remembers the gossip of the time. The old grapevine was buzzing about Malone. Talk was that one of Malone's cronies told the FBI that stolen jewels and all sorts of loot was hidden somewhere on the grounds. When questioned by a newspaper reporter back then, the Feds denied it. But '*everyone*' according to Ms. MacGregor, knew differently."

"Just like I figured." George grinned proudly. "There really *was* buried treasure."

"More like there still *is*," Ravi corrected. "It turns out that the Feds found a cache of arms, ammunition, and bootlegging paraphernalia, but they never located those jewels."

Nancy exchanged a quick glance with Ned. "So, they might still be on the property somewhere?"

"Probably. Unless, of course, they were lost when

the lake was flooded," Ravi said. "The Feds suspected that Malone's wife knew all about the jewels, but they couldn't prove it, and she never led the agents to them, even inadvertently."

Nancy felt her pulse quicken. All the pieces of the puzzle were starting to fit together.

Ned gave a low whistle. "Malone's wife," he said. "So he *did* get married."

"Isn't that amazing? I didn't think guys like Malone stayed with one woman very long," Ravi said. "He must have been different from most of them. Emily is going to flip when she hears about all of this. Old Ms. MacGregor said she'd love for Emily to come and look at her scrapbooks. She really takes pride in being part of the oral history tradition of the lake."

Ravi checked his watch. "The problem is, I won't be around to tell her. I actually have to drive back to New York today, but I'll be back early next week. Pass it all on if you see her. I'll phone her tonight and give her more details, and then figure out if we can set up a date to drive back down to see Ms. MacGregor. Emily just has to see those scrapbooks. And an interview with Ms. MacGregor would really be great for her documentary. The shock's going to blow Emily away!"

As soon as Ravi left, Nancy turned toward her friends. "He's wrong. Emily's known about this all along."

"No way!" George declared. "How could she?"

"I'm not sure—but it makes perfect sense. She's researching Prohibition era gangsters, then spends a ton of money to buy Malone's place. She must have stumbled on to something. I think she's been our prowler all along. I think she's been checking everything out, looking for anything that would lead her to Malone's wife and any kind of secret exchange of information between them."

"The letters in the attic . . . ," Ned commented.

"Right, and the plans. Though, how the FBI ever missed those, I have no idea." Nancy tried to recall the plans, then remembered the penciled arrows that had been carefully retraced with ballpoint pen.

"But the plans were stolen, Nan," George pointed out. "If she already had them why would *she* steal them. Someone else had to know about that loot."

Nancy frowned. "You've got a point. Maybe I'm moving too fast here. Maybe she knew something, but not everything."

"Then what about Jim?" George asked. "He's been acting really suspicious. Maybe all those fetishes are some kind of cover-up for his own personal treasure hunt. Or maybe he's trying to scare people away from places where he suspects the loot might be buried."

"Why would he even have a clue about where Malone would have hidden things?" Ned asked.

"Oral history," Nancy mused aloud. "It's pretty strong in the Native American community too. Ms. MacGregor might be one of the few survivors from that era, but stories get passed down. And Jim was definitely trying to locate something; remember those pins I saw on his diorama? He was pretty defensive when I asked him what they were about."

"So what's next, Nancy?" Ned asked. "I mean, even if someone finds this stuff, who's got the right to claim it? Emily, if it's on her property?"

Nancy shrugged. "I have no idea, but if we're talking about stolen goods, then I'm sure the police would be more than interested. Right now, what I want to find out is how much Emily knows." Nancy got up. "But look guys, let's keep this to ourselves for now. I don't want to let Emily know that we suspect something just yet."

"What about Bess?" George asked.

Nancy shook her head. "Let's leave her out of this for the moment. The temptation to talk about missing jewels and Malone's wife might be too much for her to handle!"

That night, Nancy couldn't sleep. She kept trying to figure out the exact connection between Mike Malone's love letters, the missing plans, Jim, and Emily. She couldn't shake the feeling that she was missing something very obvious.

Wait—the secret passage! That was it. Nancy instantly got out of bed, threw on her clothes, and tiptoed downstairs. Of *course*. If Malone had gone so far as to build a secret passageway in the cottage, there was probably another one in the main house where Emily lived. And maybe there was a secret tunnel or crawl space at the boathouse, too. Before she had been knocked out, she had noticed arrows pointing to an outside corner of the boathouse that had been recently excavated and propped up with beams. A map to another secret space?

Nancy couldn't wait until morning to check out her hunch. She slipped on her shoes, grabbed her hooded sweatshirt and a flashlight, and headed out into the cool night.

The moon was so full and bright, that she was able to make her way to the boathouse without even turning on her flashlight. As she rounded the corner of the building, a movement out on the lake caught her eye. Nancy ducked back around the side of the building and looked out onto the lake. Sure enough, a boat was silently making its way out of the bay. Then, as soon as it was a good tenth of a mile out, the motor kicked in, and the boat raced for the waters beyond Camp Moonlight.

Nancy hurried up to Emily's dock. A canoe she'd never seen before was moored to the pilings, and a damp paddle was resting in the bottom of the boat.

Nancy jumped in, loosened the rope that tied the canoe to the pier, and paddled after the other boat as quickly as she could. She had no hope of catching up to it, but she could at least follow it and find out where it was headed.

Nancy paddled furiously, keeping her eye on the speeding boat. It skimmed past Camp Moonlight, then vanished around the rocky promontory.

Nancy was so intent on following the boat that she almost didn't see an empty rowboat drifting right toward her. Where'd that come from? she wondered, paddling clear of it. As she looked back over her shoulder, an eerie sight greeted her eyes. The shallow harbor of Camp Moonlight was a ghostly flotilla of drifting boats: canoes, rowboats, flat-bottomed dinghies, and kayaks.

Nancy froze with her paddle in the air. How did all those boats get loose from their moorings? They had been tied up on the beach the day before, when she and Ned had run into Steve Delmonico. Someone must have cut all those boats loose. But why?

Just then, a dinghy drifted next to her. It banged into the side of her canoe, practically tipping it over. Nancy struggled to keep the boat upright.

Suddenly a male figure rose up out of the dinghy and let out a loud cry. He lunged toward Nancy, tipping her canoe. Nancy struggled to stay upright, but didn't have a chance against the man's strength.

Nancy was thrust into the cold, dark water. She tried to grab on to the edge of her boat, but a booted foot kicked her hand, sending a jolt of pain up her arm. She let go of the boat, and sank into the depths of the lake.

15

The Past Revealed

Nancy's head stung from where she hit the side of the boat, but she was conscious. With a few strong kicks, she surfaced right under the canoe, coughing and sputtering. She took advantage of the air pocket between the canoe and the water, and gulped down a couple of deep breaths of air. She had to right the canoe. Nancy pushed with both hands, but it wouldn't budge. It felt like someone was holding it down over her head.

Someone was trying to drown her! Nancy panicked for a second. She then gulped down another breath of air and dove deeper underwater, swimming away from the boat. With a thrust of her legs, she propelled herself up out of the water, clear of the canoe.

But not clear of the man in the dinghy. Before Nancy could orient herself, a paddle crashed down on her head. Everything went dark.

The next thing Nancy sensed was something cold, rough, and damp against her bare arms. She tried to open her eyes, but her head was pounding, and her eyes felt stuck shut.

"Take it easy," a man's voice whispered. "And be quiet!"

Nancy couldn't tell if his words signaled a warning or a threat. She felt a wave of nausea and began to cough. Rough hands lifted her head up. Nancy touched the ground. It was damp sand. She was on a beach. The memory of what had happened on the lake rushed back to her: the flotilla of boats, the male figure that towered out of a dinghy and tried to drown her. But how had she landed here? And where was *here*?

Finally, Nancy was able to open her eyes. They were sticky and they stung. "Wh-what happened?" she muttered, looking up.

It was Jim! Shock and fear made her scramble to her feet. Her knees felt weak, but she forced herself to stand and face him. She quickly scanned the unfamiliar beach, looking for something to use to defend herself. "It was you who just tried to drown me!"

Jim gave an infuriating laugh. "I don't believe you.

If I were going to drown you, why would I drag you all the way to this beach?"

Nancy stared at him. "Oh, so you just happened to turn up, and—" Nancy stopped midsentence. Jim's hunting knife was hanging from his belt. How had he retrieved it from the Fayne cottage?

Jim followed her eyes. "Look, this is a hunting knife. I use it for cutting rope or branches. Not people." He lifted both hands, open-palmed, in a gesture of peace.

"How did you get it back?" Nancy asked.

Jim's face registered pure confusion. "Back?" He touched his knife. "I never lost it."

"I found it yesterday morning on a platform in the woods, right near one of your rock piles."

"Oh, you mean up in the blind. That's not my blind. That's the Lawrence-Joneses' setup. For so-called nature lovers," Jim said, mockingly. "What they're really doing is messing up the environment."

Nancy studied Jim. Had she been wrong all along? "So, then, what exactly *are* you doing here? It's the middle of the night, Jim."

A funny smile played around his lips. "I could ask you the same question—and I have a feeling we'd have a similar answer," he said. "There have been some weird goings-on around the lake at night over the past few months. Dredging at night, digging in

141

the woods. I've been trying to figure out if someone's been out to disturb the sites that some of our Native American archeologists have turned up; we've found some tribal artifacts."

"The map locators on your diorama," Nancy blurted. Suddenly, it all started to become clear. Jim's weird behavior began to make sense. "But what about all those fetishes and cairns?"

"I've been trying to mark places that have sacred meaning to our people. If we win that court battle, we'll have a right to a narrow strip of land that runs through all the property on this side of the lake. I've been trying to blaze a rough trail through some of the more sacred spots. Maybe our tribal elders will want them kept free of visitors. But I'm hoping they'll want to create some sort of self-guided educational walk so that people in the area will know the true history of the native people who lived here." As Jim spoke, his eyes brightened, and his face filled with passion.

Nancy had really misjudged him. "So, after all this scouting around at night, what have you found? And who just tried to do me in?" Nancy rubbed her head. "And why?"

Jim put his finger to his lips, motioning for Nancy to lower her voice. "I'm not sure why, but obviously your own 'scouting around' seems to be making someone very nervous. I don't know what you've been looking for, but I suspect you're close to finding it. Here, come with me," Jim said, motioning for her to follow him.

Nancy took a moment to orient herself. She'd finally stopped shivering, but she was still cold and felt a little sick. She looked to her left and realized she was on the other side of the promontory that formed the western border of Camp Moonlight. The shallow beach was semicircular in shape, with the western part of the camp on the left, and a lower, wooded strip of land on the right. There was no dock or pier. The beach ran right up to the edge of the woods. "What is this place?" she asked Jim.

"State park. It's small, but it gives hikers access to the water." He started up the beach. Nancy followed him. Jim moved quickly, but quietly. Together they climbed up to the crest of the wooded hill. Jim dropped to a low crouch, and Nancy followed suit. He led her behind a boulder, then motioned for her to look below.

Nancy peeked around the rock. There was another moonlit beach hemmed in by trees. Clearly visible in the moonlight, a woman stood knee-deep in the lake. As Nancy watched, a man in scuba gear broke the surface of the lake, just a few yards away from the woman. He was holding some sort of box. It was dripping with weeds and muck, but even from where she stood, Nancy heard the woman cheer.

"We found it!" she cried happily.

"Emily Griffen!" Nancy whispered, slowly shaking

her head. So Nancy had guessed right. Emily knew about the treasure all along. Somehow, she had figured out where to find it.

"And that nasty Dale Weyrhausen," Jim murmured.

"Nasty?" Nancy repeated.

"That's the polite word for him," Jim declared hotly. "That guy and his partner have been breaking every rule about dredging in the lake for artifacts. The police turn a blind eye to it; either they don't believe these guys ever turn up anything of value, or they just don't care. It's illegal to take anything from the lake, whether it's tribal, or not. Meanwhile, Dale and his partner have also been raiding some of the small Native American sites I mentioned earlier. They look dumb, but these guys are smart enough to sell anything valuable someplace far from here. They bring all the general junk to Timothy's, in town. Tim's another one who turns a blind eye, though the stuff they bring him is really only of value to junk collectors."

"Let's get a closer look," Nancy said, slipping past Jim and quietly moving down the hill. The brush was thick, and Nancy was able to creep within a few yards of the pair. They had carried the box to the shore, and were both bent over it.

"What's she doing?" Jim asked.

Nancy couldn't believe her eyes. "She has a key!" she whispered excitedly, turning to Jim. Had Emily found the key in one of the trunks? Or maybe that's what was under that floorboard in the pantry?

"Hey, what's going on there?!" Jim whispered loudly to Nancy.

Nancy's whirled around. While Emily knelt in front of the box, trying to work the key in the lock, another man had slipped behind her. He was holding a piece of driftwood in his hands, and was brandishing it over her head. It was Kevin, Dale's partner. Where had he come from?!

Nancy didn't give it a second thought. She sprang into action. "Emily, watch out!" she yelled, tackling Kevin from behind.

Kevin fell flat on his face, but Dale was quick. He grabbed Emily's arm and the box and began dragging them toward the woods.

Kevin quickly recovered from Nancy's surprise attack. He rolled over and tried to pin her down, but Jim raced to her rescue. He yanked Kevin off Nancy. "You tried to kill her once tonight. You're not going to get a second chance." He hauled back and punched Kevin in the nose, knocking him out cold.

Nancy scrambled to her feet. "Dale has Emily!" she said, breathlessly. "What do you think, is it safe to leave him?" She gestured toward Kevin.

"He's down for the count," Jim said, then followed Nancy into the woods. They could hear Dale and Emily crashing through the bushes just up ahead.

"Let me go!" Emily was shouting.

"Give me the key, and I'll let you go!" Dale snarled.

Nancy stopped in her tracks. She motioned silently for Jim to go in the opposite direction so that the two of them could circle around the pair.

Jim nodded, put his fingers to his lips, and let out an owl's cry. Then he raised three fingers. Nancy grinned. A signal.

A few minutes later, "Hooo! Hooo! Hooo! Hooo!" rang through the forest.

Emily and Dale were still shouting at each other. Nancy counted to three, then burst through the bushes.

"You again?" Dale snapped, but Jim had grabbed him from behind.

"Yeah, us again!" Jim said. He looked toward the spot where Emily had stood only moments ago. "Hey," he said, surprised, "what happened to Emily?"

"Maybe she doesn't want rescuing!" Dale taunted.

Nancy could hear Emily stumbling through the forest. "Jim, I'll follow her. Why don't you bring Dale down to the beach? As soon as I get Emily, I'll call the police." Jim nodded.

Nancy followed Emily's trail. Just ahead, at the clearing on the edge of Camp Moonlight, she saw Emily half running, half limping down the dirt driveway of the camp, with the box tucked under her arm. It looked like she was heading toward the line of forest between her property and Steve Delmonico's.

Nancy caught up to her easily. She grabbed Emily's arm, and the box went flying. It landed hard on a rock, popping open and spilling its contents.

Precious stones of every sort glistened in the moonlight. There were ruby bracelets, diamond pendants, loose stones, all sorts of gold rings, a fortune's worth of gold coins, and finally, a small oval locket.

Nancy stooped down over the box, but Emily tried to kick her away. "Stay away! That's mine!" she cried, as Nancy warded off the blows. Emily sank down beside Nancy and began to sob.

"Just because you found it doesn't mean it's yours, Emily," Nancy said. "You didn't even find it on your land. Even if you had, this is stolen property. The FBI looked for this stuff all through the nineteen-thirties and never found it. Obviously, the place where Malone buried it got flooded by the lake. It looks like he planned it that way," Nancy added. She thought for a moment. Malone did have the foreknowledge of the hydroelectric project. He planned that his treasure would be buried where no one but he or his wife could eventually find it. Nancy wondered about whatever happened to Malone . . . why he never came back when his jail time was finished . . .

Just then the wail of sirens pierced through the night. Emily looked up, clearly panicked. She tried to gather up the jewels. Nancy stopped her. "I wouldn't try to avoid the police on this, Emily. Or you might end up in some real trouble here."

Suddenly George, Ned, and Bess broke through the bushes. The beams of their flashlights danced across Steve Delmonico's dirt drive. "Nancy—thank goodness, you're okay!" Ned cried.

"I heard a noise and thought there was a ghost," Bess admitted shyly. "I grabbed a poker that I've been keeping in the bedroom, and went downstairs. Then I saw you walking toward the boathouse. When I saw you set off in a boat, I woke everyone up."

"But by the time we got outside, your boat was gone, and there were hundreds of canoes every-where!" George pointed out.

"What's with Emily?" Ned asked, then he spotted the jewels. "Man! That's Malone's treasure!"

"All that *jewelry*!" Bess gasped.

"It's not Malone's treasure. It belongs to me!" Emily suddenly cried, grabbing a locket and jumping up. But the state police were coming up the driveway.

Just then, Steve Delmonico came barreling out of his house. "Caught you!" he shouted, as the police got out of their car and walked toward the little group gathered by the edge of the driveway.

"What's going on here? What are you kids up to?" asked one of the officers. Then he spotted the jewels. "Omigosh, is that what I think it is?"

His partner shoved back his hat. "I don't know

what *you* think it is, but I'd say that's a pretty valuable cache of jewelry. Does it belong to any of you?"

"Me!" Emily said, two little red spots burning on her cheeks. She stood square to the policemen. "This locket belonged to my great-grandmother, which makes it mine."

"Your great-grandmother?" Nancy asked.

"Mike Malone's wife, Nellie," Emily said, with a defiant toss of her head.

"Well, I'll be," Steve Delmonico exclaimed, looking at Emily with new respect. "That's why you were so hot to buy that property. So you could find those famous missing jewels. Congratulations! You've hit the jackpot."

"Wait a minute," Nancy said, talking directly to the troopers. "She found this box buried just offshore of the state park—not on her land." The troopers turned to Emily.

"You're wrong. It's mine," Emily insisted. "Yes, I found it there, but it's still mine."

"Hmm. You kids had nothing to do with all those boats being vandalized, though?" one of the troopers asked.

"Doesn't matter. I won't press charges," Steve said, with a new-found deference to Emily that Nancy personally found revolting.

"Then I will," Nancy said. "None of us had anything to do with those boats. If you row over to the state park beach, though, you'll find Jim Whitehall-Evans. He's standing guard over Dale and Kevin. They assaulted me and Emily, and they're the ones who vandalized Mr. Delmonico's property."

The trooper got on his walkie-talkie and radioed the lake patrol police to pick up the two men and bring Jim back to town.

As soon as the trooper was off the radio, Emily asked, "So, I can keep the box and its contents?"

"Uh . . . no, miss. First of all, it seems that it *is* stolen property. Second, I need more proof of your relationship to Malone. If your story is true, you'll have to prove it in court. Meanwhile, I'll have to confiscate this. If you come in to the barracks with us, we'll give you a receipt for its contents."

Emily looked devastated.

Just then, the troopers' radio squawked. Lake patrol had picked up Jim and the two men. They would book the two guys and get Jim's statement about what happened.

"I should go into town too. You'll probably need my account of what went on tonight," Nancy volunteered, putting her hand on Emily's arm. Emily started to pull away, then relaxed. Tears started rolling down her cheeks.

"I'd appreciate the company," Emily said quietly.

Nancy turned toward her friends. "Maybe you guys could follow in my car? When Emily's finished down there, we can give her a lift home." Ned, Bess, and George agreed.

"So, now, what's the whole story, Nancy?" Bess asked early the next afternoon. "I can't bear the suspense one minute longer!"

The night before, after brief questioning, Emily had decided to stay in a motel in town. She would go to court in the morning to stake her claim to the property she'd found. Nancy's friends waited outside while Emily and Nancy spoke to the troopers. Everyone except for Emily had arrived home just as dawn was breaking over the lake.

They were all too tired to talk, but Nancy had promised to relate Emily's story over brunch.

A light rain was falling, and the foursome was devouring pancakes at the table in the family room. The deck doors were open, and a fresh, damp breeze blew through the room.

"It turns out," Nancy started, "that Malone's wife was visiting relatives with her infant son at the time of Malone's arrest here at the lake. The missing letters from that packet I found, revealed the fact that he'd buried a boxful of jewels and gold on the far end of what was then still his property. He purposely buried the box in a place where it would be offshore once the lake was flooded."

"Wow,. his planning worked," George marveled,

pouring herself some orange juice. She passed the container to Bess. "The FBI was never able to find it."

"Apparently, his wife knew all along where it was. She was supposed to be able to retrieve it if she needed the money. But the FBI kept too close a watch on her, just like Ms. MacGregor told Ravi."

"But where does Emily come into all this? And how come she didn't know about being a Malone until recently?" Bess asked. "Or did she?"

Nancy shook her head. "When Emily's great-grandmother died on the West Coast, her son was adopted and given a new name by his adoptive parents."

"Griffen?" Ned surmised.

"Yes," Nancy continued. "This woman's son was Emily's grandfather. By the time Emily Griffen was born, no one had a clue that she was actually a Malone."

"Until Emily researched her documentary," Bess concluded. "It's such a romantic story."

"It's a sad story. And I don't know if Emily will ever be able to claim the property. There must be insurance questions. The only thing that she seems to be able to prove legally belongs to her is the locket, which has her great-grandmother's photo in it. She found another photo of her during her research."

"But how did she know about the letters? And what about that plan?" George asked.

"I'm not sure. She said she knew there had been letters of some sort, because she read that the FBI began intercepting twice-a-week mail from Malone to his wife when he was in prison. Emily learned about the secret passage from plans she found in the main house. The letters inside mentioned a plan for where the treasure was hidden, and the boathouse. She never did find out what the boathouse had to do with anything. Maybe Malone originally intended to hide his stolen goods there."

For a moment they all sat silently, listening to the drum of rain on the deck. "It *is* a sad story," Bess said. "Finding out who your family is—and then learning that you have a relative who was a big-time gangster."

Nancy nodded. "Emily's having a hard time with that. But I think in the long run it's going to work in her favor. Imagine doing a documentary about your own great-grandfather!"

Suddenly, there was a knock on the back door. "Anyone home?" a high-pitched woman's voice called in a British accent.

"Oh, no!" Bess slumped down in her chair. "The Lawrence-Joneses. Now what did we do?"

"We can't tell them we aren't here," George said, getting up and going to the door. "Hi, come on in!" she said brightly.

Nancy heard a clear note of insincerity in George's voice.

"I hope we aren't bothering you," Millicent said, walking into the family room. She eyed the remains of the friends' brunch and grinned. "I think maybe this peace offering is coming at an odd time, right Caspar?" She handed George a large covered cake dish. It had a see-through lid, and inside was a fluffy, pink layer cake.

Her husband shuffled in after her, looking distinctly shy. "I don't think the timing matters. Actually, we wanted to apologize to you kids. We've been blaming you for all the problems we've been having. It turns out that with one exception, you've had nothing to do with any of it. Those awful men, Dale and Kevin from that hauling company, seem to have been behind most of our problems."

"Oh, so you heard about all that already?" Nancy said, somewhat surprised.

"It was on the police scanner; we listen to it a lot. It's the only way we know what's going on around here. We hear sirens. We see lights, but we never know if someone's been murdered, or what!" Millicent complained.

George motioned for the couple to sit down.

"No, thank you," Caspar said. "We've got a lot of work to do today. There's a whole raft of eider ducks one of the Audubon folks spotted over in Baily's cove. That's clear across the lake! We can't stay. But I do want to apologize for thinking the worst of you kids."

154

"Apologies accepted," Nancy said gracefully.

"Good. Because I thought you might like this souvenir of your stay here." He handed Nancy an envelope.

She opened it. Inside was a glossy black-and-white photo. Nancy winced. "Oh, I don't believe this," she groaned. It showed Nancy wide-eyed and stumbling, about to fall facedown into a pile of thorns. It was the shot she had triggered when she tripped over the Lawrence-Joneses' night photo setup a few nights back.

Ned, Bess, and George gathered around. Ned and Bess couldn't help but laugh.

George gave Nancy a friendly pat on the back. "Nancy, I can't believe it. For once, you really look like you lost it!" She smiled.

For a moment Nancy was mortified, then she began to laugh too. "I do make the funniest-looking screech owl anyone's ever seen!"

3 1221 08251 0582

NOW ON AUDIO!

The Original HARDY BOYS and NANCY DREW MYSTERIES

Available for the first time
EVER as audiobooks!

Listen to the mysterious adventures of these clever teen detectives.

Nancy Drew® #1:
The Secret of the Old Clock
0-8072-0754-3

The Hardy Boys® #1:
The Tower Treasure
0-8072-0766-7

Nancy Drew® #2:
The Hidden Staircase
0-8072-0757-8

The Hardy Boys® #2:
The House on the Cliff
0-8072-0769-1

Each program: Unabridged • 2 cassettes
$18.00/$28.00C

LISTENING LIBRARY

LISTENING LIBRARY is a registered trademark of Random House, Inc.
Nancy Drew Hardy Boys and all related characters ©® S&S, Inc.

available wherever books and audiobooks are sold

to www.listeninglibrary.com to listen to audio excerpts from these brain-teasing mysteries.